FIELD OF SCREAMS

ALSO BY JOEL A. SUTHERLAND

The Haunted series

The Nightmare Next Door

Field of Screams

Ghosts Never Die

Night of the Living Dolls

Field of Screams

Joel A. Sutherland

sourcebooks
young readers

Published by Sourcebooks Young Readers, an imprint of Sourcebooks Kids
P.O. Box 4410, Naperville, Illinois 60567-4410
(630) 961-3900
sourcebookskids.com

Originally published in 2019 in Canada by Scholastic Canada Ltd.

Library of Congress Cataloging-in-Publication Data

Names: Sutherland, Joel A., author.
Title: Field of screams / Joel A. Sutherland.
Description: Naperville, Illinois : Sourcebooks Young Readers, 2020. |
  Series: [Haunted ; book 2] | Audience: Ages 8-12. | Audience: Grades 4-6. |
  Summary: "Can Darius and Ryan escape the haunted corn maze before
  it's too late?"-- Provided by publisher.
Identifiers: LCCN 2020015753 | (trade paperback)
Subjects: CYAC: Maze puzzles--Fiction. | Cousins--Fiction. | Horror stories.
Classification: LCC PZ7.1.S8825 Fie 2020 | DDC [Fic]--dc23
LC record available at https://lccn.loc.gov/2020015753

This product conforms to all applicable CPSC and CPSIA standards.

Source of Production: Sheridan Books, Chelsea, Michigan, United States
Date of Production: May 2020
Run Number: 5018758

Printed and bound in the United States of America.
SB 10 9 8 7 6 5 4 3 2 1

For my Charles, who can always find his way out of a maze, even if he's torn between using his grandpa's "keep your hand on the left wall" trick or just winging it.

CHAPTER 1

THE GIRL STOOD AT THE entrance of the corn maze and hesitated. Her eyes were full of curiosity, but her brow was furrowed with concern. She looked like she wasn't sure whether she actually wanted to enter.

A bloodcurdling scream pierced the cool autumn air. The girl flinched and hugged herself, both for warmth and comfort. The sound had come from deep within the maze. It sounded like someone was dying.

The moon was full and bright, but a long, lean shadow cloaked the girl in darkness. The shadow was cast by a hideous scarecrow that towered above her. Its face—carved into the flesh of a ripe pumpkin—leered down at her. The scarecrow held a large scythe that was planted in the dirt beside the entrance to the maze. The blade gleamed in the moonlight and was positioned over the entrance like a gate...or worse, like a guillotine, ready to fall and decapitate whoever was brave enough—or foolish enough—to enter.

Whether the girl fell into the brave camp or the foolish camp was unclear. She entered the maze, took one final look over her shoulder at the farm, and then the corn swallowed her up.

She walked deeper and deeper into the maze, picking up her pace until she was jogging. The more time that passed without something—anything—happening, the more nervous she became. It was plainly obvious the corn maze was a bad place filled with bad things, so what were they waiting for? Why hadn't the bad people, the bad things, shown themselves?

Left, right, left, right, left, left, left, right... The girl soon became turned around and disoriented. She didn't know which direction to go. She started to panic, fear furrowing her brow and making her whip her head anxiously from side to side.

Another scream tore through the air, much closer this time. The girl jumped and turned a corner without peering around the cornstalks' edge and came face-to-face with a scarecrow. Unlike the scarecrow at the entrance, this one walked. It smiled with malice. It was alive. And it lunged for the girl.

She screamed, adding her own note of terror to the night, and ran around the scarecrow. It tried to grab her with its straw hands but narrowly missed her shoulders.

The girl no longer jogged. She ran. Ran as fast as her legs would carry her. She sped straight down the path, came to a dead end, and made a quick turn to her left.

A tall man wearing a dirty hockey mask and holding a chainsaw blocked her way. He gripped the chainsaw's cord, preparing to give it a hard yank.

The girl skidded to a frantic stop, turned, and ran in the other direction. Before she'd gone more than a few feet, a clawed hand reached out from the cornstalks beside her. She shrieked and didn't pause to take a better look, but the creature's face appeared to be covered in fur, and it had large, gnashing teeth.

But then the girl turned another corner and came face-to-face with something that stopped her dead in her tracks. It was a man wearing a dirty butcher's apron. He gripped a long carving knife that he ran back and forth against a sharpener with a sound more grating than nails on a chalkboard. But the thing that commanded the girl's full attention was the man's head. It wasn't human. Instead, on top of his large shoulders, he had a pig's head.

"Oink, oink, oink," the pig man said as he sharpened his knife with a *shink-shink-shink*.

The girl couldn't move—she was rooted to the ground in terror—and the time for screaming had passed. She raised her hands to the sides of her head and closed her eyes tight, unable to watch what was to happen next.

And because of my annoying little sister, Grace, I didn't see what happened next, either.

She grabbed the remote control out of my hand and quickly changed the channel. Before I knew what had happened I was watching Mickey and Minnie Mouse in their clubhouse preparing a picnic. "Hot diggity dog," Mickey said as he put a pack of hot dogs in his basket.

"Hey!" I shouted. "I was watching that."

"It was too scary," Grace countered.

We were sitting side by side in Mom's bed, watching the TV. I swiped the remote back from

Grace—she tried to stop me, but I was much bigger and faster than her.

"No, Darius, no!" she wailed.

"Cover your eyes," I said, and changed the channel back. Grace would be fine.

And so was the girl in the corn maze. She was back out in the farmyard, safe and sound, walking with a couple of friends, their arms linked together and laughing.

"For the twelfth year in a row," a man with an overly dramatic spooky voice narrated, "Wight Farm transforms into Fall Fright at sundown every Friday, Saturday, and Sunday in September and October. Are you brave enough to enter our infamous corn maze? Less than twenty-five minutes from downtown Kelowna. Prepare to scream!"

The screen cut to black for a second, and then an ad for a local company called DIY Dolls with an annoyingly catchy jingle came on. It was a jarring contradiction to the Fall Fright ad.

"Is it safe to look now?" Grace asked peeked through her fingers.

I didn't answer. I was thinking about Fall Fright. I used to love it and had gone with my dad every year since I could remember. But now seeing the ad left me feeling lonely and hollow. I doubted I'd ever go to Fall Fright again. It was just one of many things I used to do with Dad that were forever in the past.

The ad that had just played was the same one as they'd aired the year before. Same girl, same corn maze, same monsters. They hadn't even bothered to update the voice-over at the end— this was actually the thirteenth year in a row Wight Farm was transforming into Fall Fright, not the twelfth.

I turned to Grace to tell her it was safe to look now, but she was already happily humming along to the DIY Dolls jingle. I laughed and considered pointing out that the images of doll parts— torsos, limbs, and heads—sitting in buckets to

7

be shipped to amateur doll makers across the country was slightly more disturbing than Fall Fright's ad, but decided to keep that observation to myself. Like all little sisters, Grace could be annoying, but she was much less so when she was happy and occupied.

Maybe the TV station had made a mistake and accidentally played last year's commercial. Maybe Fall Fright wasn't actually happening this year. I sighed, knowing that was wishful thinking. Aunt Kelly and my cousin, Ryan, were coming to town for a weekend visit, and I was pretty sure Ryan would want to go to Fall Fright. Dad had taken us every year because our moms hated the place and Ryan's dad... Well, Ryan's dad hadn't been the fatherly type for years. So Ryan would probably want to go, and I couldn't think of a single excuse—other than the real reason, which I didn't want to admit—why I didn't want to go.

Maybe Ryan wouldn't ask to go. Maybe he'd think we had outgrown it. Maybe something else had come up, and he and my aunt were about to call my mom to cancel the visit. Maybe I'd get to enjoy a quiet, peaceful weekend free from scarecrows and masked maniacs and pig men butchers and other horrors.

Ding, dong!

No such luck.

CHAPTER 2

IT TOOK ME A MINUTE to get moving, but once I started down the staircase, I began to grow excited again. My aunt and cousin had moved three years ago, and the last time I'd seen them was before the holidays, for my dad's funeral. Although it had been ten months, it was still hard to think about it.

I reached the front hallway and forced a smile.

Mom had already let our guests in. "Hey, Ryan," I said.

He dropped his backpack at his feet and nodded. "What's up, Darius?"

We high-fived and gave each other a brief, backslapping hug.

"Good to see you, Aunt Kelly." I gave her a quick hug, too.

"You've gotten so tall since the last time I saw you," she said. "How are you holding up?"

"I'm fine?" I said, hating that I'd said it like a question. But I'd grown tired of answering questions like that over the past ten months.

"I don't know how he keeps growing," Mom said, picking up on my discomfort and redirecting the conversation. "He eats like a bird."

"Really?" Aunt Kelly said. She placed a hand on Ryan's shoulder. "Not this one. He eats like a pig."

The image of the pig man butcher from the Fall Fright ad flashed through my head, and I forced it out.

"Yeah, but your cooking doesn't count,"

11

Ryan said. "Nothing but health food, free of gluten, sugar, and red meat. Free of flavor, too. Please tell me I can have a cheeseburger while I'm here."

I opened my mouth to say, "Sure," but didn't want to upset my aunt the moment she'd arrived.

"It's fine," she said with an exaggerated sigh. "You can splurge this weekend, Ryan. But as soon as we're back home—"

"I know—gluten-free, sugar-free, red-meat-free, taste-free."

"You got it. Except for taste-free. Contrary to popular opinion, my cooking is delicious."

"Why don't you boys head upstairs?" Mom said. "It's late, and Ryan has had a long drive."

"That will give us a chance to catch up," Aunt Kelly told my mom.

"After I put Grace to bed," Mom said. "Speaking of Grace, where is she?"

"She's watching *Mickey Mouse Clubhouse* in your room," I said.

"I thought I heard some yelling a few minutes ago," Mom said, eyeing me.

"Oh, that? It's all good," I said, waving a hand casually in the air. "We just wanted to watch different things, that's all. C'mon, Ryan. Let's go to my room."

We said good night to our moms, went upstairs, and closed my bedroom door.

"You okay sleeping on the air mattress?" I asked. Mom and I had inflated it earlier, then covered it with a sheet, a blanket, and a pillow.

"No problem." Ryan placed his bag on the floor and lay down on the mattress. It squeaked and groaned a little under his weight. He stretched his arms out, tucked them under the back of his head, and closed his eyes.

Was he going to sleep, just like that?

"Just because my mom said we should, doesn't mean we need to go to sleep right away," I said.

"I know," Ryan said with a yawn. "It's nice to

lay here and chill, you know? I don't want to use my brain at all."

I thought we'd watch a movie on my laptop, play some video games, or at least talk for a while.

"Sure. I get it," I said. "So what do you want to do tomorrow?"

Ryan opened his eyes and sat up. "Well, since you asked, I was thinking it would be fun to go to Fall Fright."

I instantly regretted asking.

I didn't answer at first, so Ryan added, "You know, for old times' sake?"

I frowned and nodded, knowing I had to say something sooner rather than later or else the rest of the weekend might be intensely awkward. "Yeah, sure. Old times' sake."

"Is that cool?"

"Absolutely," I said. "It's cool."

"That weird old guy still running the place? The one who walks around the farm wearing that nasty straw hat?"

"Old Man Wight," I said. "Obsessed with his corn maze." It's what all the kids at school always said. No one actually knew if the old guy in the straw hat was the Wight who ran the farm, but everyone did know to keep their distance from the guy. He gave off a weird vibe, but not the kind you went to Fall Fright for. "Yeah, he's still there—older and creepier each year."

Ryan smiled. "Too funny. Well, sounds like we've got a plan."

"Yeah, sure," I said.

"You positive you want to go to Fall Fright?"

"I said 'yeah, sure,' didn't I?"

"Yeah..." Ryan said, the word drawn out.

"I'm sure I want to go." I sighed, disappointed by how crabby I knew I sounded, but I figured a white lie might be the best way to keep things from getting any more awkward than they already were.

"All right," Ryan said. His tone was mostly confused, but also sounded a little offended.

Wishing I could disappear into a deep hole for an hour or two, I decided to change the subject. "Are you into *Kill Screen*?"

"The video game that can't be beat, right?"

"Yeah, that's the one. But I doubt that's true," I said. "I have this theory that the people who made the game started that rumor just to create some buzz. Anyway, I've got a copy. It's really fun."

Ryan shrugged. "I don't really play games much anymore."

"Serious? We used to spend hours gaming."

He shrugged again.

"Okay," I said, deciding to plow on. "Have you seen the latest episode of *Screamers*?"

Ryan didn't answer.

"Don't tell me you don't watch it anymore!" I said.

He smiled sheepishly.

I laughed, grabbed an old toy from the shelf beside my bed, and threw it at him. He caught it and laughed back.

"Did moving away turn you into a big baby or something?" I asked.

"Did staying here make you lose your mind?" He held up the toy. "This is Tommy Talks. It's a collector's item now. I sold mine for forty bucks online last year."

"You serious?" I took Tommy Talks back from him much more gently than I'd thrown it. "Grace has a Sadie Sees, too. Maybe I could sell them together as a pair."

"Don't get your hopes up. They mass-produced Sadie Sees, so they're pretty much worthless."

"Oh well. Guess I'll hang on to you for a while." I placed Tommy Talks back on the shelf.

"You sure you want to go to Fall Fright?" Ryan asked again. "Last chance to back out without *too* much teasing from me."

I stared at the ceiling and nodded, unsure whether or not he could see me. Maybe that was for the best. My cheeks felt flushed. "Nah, we can go. It's just, I've never gone without..." *Without my dad*, I thought. "Without a group of, like, three or four people."

We were both silent for a moment. There was a low rumble that sounded a lot like distant thunder. I wondered if Ryan had bought my excuse.

"Here's an idea," Ryan said. "You can bring Tommy Talks. That'll make three, plus you'll have him for comfort in case you get too scared."

"Ha, ha," I said. "I'll be fine."

But would I be? I wasn't so sure.

Ryan yawned, which I took as a sign that he was growing tired again.

I said good night, turned off the light, and stared at my darkened ceiling for hours while I failed to fall asleep.

CHAPTER 3

ALTHOUGH I WOKE UP THE next morning feeling exhausted and a little down, I immediately felt my luck might be beginning to change. Outside I could hear rain pounding on the roof and lashing the window. I opened the blinds and looked out at the street in front of the house. The sun was completely blotted out by the dark clouds that clogged the sky.

"Do you think Fall Fright will be closed tonight?" Ryan asked.

The rain was coming down in sheets. Water

rushed along the street, carrying leaves and twigs. The sky was the color of a waterlogged corpse.

"Probably," I said, trying to keep any note of relief out of my tone. "Most of the attractions are outside."

"Phones in the basket," Mom said as soon as we entered the kitchen. It was one of the rules she'd made me agree to when I'd gotten my own phone: no phones at mealtimes. She'd made scrambled eggs and bacon—the real kind, not that fake bacon made from turkey I liked to call *facon*. Ryan ate like it was his last meal. Aunt Kelly tried to act like she didn't care, but I caught her shooting him disgusted looks every now and again while she ate half a grapefruit with no sugar. We talked about the day's plans as the rain continued falling.

We excused ourselves and went to the basement, and Ryan agreed to play a few rounds of *Kill Screen* even though video games weren't really his thing anymore. Grace came down at the precise moment that a hideous ghost with bloody teeth and black eyes jumped out of the shadows with a high-pitched shriek. Grace screamed louder than the ghost and flew back up the stairs, ending our gaming session.

Ryan and I felt bad so we went upstairs and played three billion rounds of Grace's favorite game, Hungry Hungry Hippos (it might have been more like six or seven games, but it felt like a lot more) and followed that up with five hours of duck, duck, goose (probably only ten minutes). Mom called us for lunch, we put our phones in the basket, we ate, and still it continued to rain.

I didn't know what else to do to keep Ryan entertained. We turned on the TV in the family room and had a boring conversation while we watched a boring show.

"I'm cold. Are you cold?"

"I don't know. Not really, I guess."

"Weird. I'm cold. Don't know how you aren't."

"Anything interesting happen at school so far this year?"

"Nah. You?"

"Nah. Well, actually, a couple of weeks ago my math teacher told us not to disturb him because he had some 'important work' to take care of. Little did he know that his computer was hooked up to the projector and he legit watched *Titanic* for, like, twenty minutes before he realized his mistake."

"No kidding."

"Yeah. It was really funny. Guess you had to be there."

"I guess."

"Yeah."

"You sure you aren't cold?"

"Pretty sure."

"I'm cold."

And on and on and on. I felt like I was getting dumber by the minute.

"What's that?" Ryan asked out of the blue.

I had a feeling I knew what he'd spotted before I followed his gaze. He was looking at the fireplace mantel.

"My dad's hiking gloves," I said. "And his urn."

"Whoa, really?"

I nodded.

"I had no idea he was cremated. I guess I assumed he'd be buried sometime after the winter."

I shook my head.

"Sorry I brought it up."

"It's okay," I said. "Mom hates cemeteries. She wanted Dad to be close, at least for a while. We've talked about taking his urn to Rose Valley Park to spread his ashes, but..." I spread my hands to my sides.

"I get it," Ryan said. "It must be tough to move on." He suddenly cupped a hand over his mouth, then slid it up to his forehead as if he was sick and taking his own temperature. "Oh, man. Is that why you don't seem to want to go to Fall Fright? Because your dad used to go with us?"

I sighed with every intention of answering but found I was tongue-tied.

"I'm sorry, Dare," Ryan said. "Forget about it. Let's do something else tonight even if it does stop raining—"

"Everything reminds me of Dad," I said without thinking. "Everything. Every room in this house and every piece of furniture in it. Every TV show we used to watch together, every trail we used to hike, every holiday he misses, every meal he's not there..."

I looked at the urn, at what was left of my dad, and made a decision. A small one, but a decision all the same—and maybe it was about time I did.

"I can't keep avoiding things because I'm afraid," I said. "I used to love Fall Fright. We should go." I nodded. "I want to go."

Ryan nodded. "Okay. And if you don't want to stay long, that's fine with me."

Mom called us for dinner. Although I felt good about the decision I'd made, I was also thankful for the distraction.

We joined Aunt Kelly, Mom, and Grace in the kitchen.

"Phones in the—"

"Basket," Ryan finished for my mom. "Mine's upstairs. I've already learned not to bring it with me for meals."

Both Mom and Aunt Kelly looked impressed. Mom shot me a somewhat disapproving look as I put my phone in the basket.

"What?" I said. It wasn't like I was breaking her rule.

Mom had made chicken noodle soup and ham and cheese sandwiches, plus what looked like a hummus and veggie sandwich for my aunt. I crumbled some crackers over my soup, picked up my spoon, and dug in. It was hot, salty, and delicious—a perfect meal on a rainy day.

"I know you want to go to Fall Fright," Mom

said as we ate, "but do you have a backup plan if it doesn't stop raining?"

"Maybe we could go to the movies?" I asked Ryan.

"Yeah, maybe," he said through a mouthful of ham sandwich. There was a smear of yellow mustard on his cheek. He had already half-finished his sandwich. I had the feeling he was afraid his mother would suddenly yank it away and insist he eat hummus instead.

"Is there anything good playing?" Mom asked.

"A couple of horror movies," Ryan said. "One looks all right: *Time to Die*. It's about a scientist who can't stop time traveling back to the day he was murdered, but every time he goes back he's killed in a different, gruesome way."

"Wait a minute," I said. "How does he travel back in time if...he's already dead?"

Ryan opened his mouth, but then seemed to realize he had no idea how to answer that.

"*Time to Die* is rated R," Aunt Kelly said with a disapproving look.

"You're right," Ryan said with a sigh. "Guess I'll have to wait until it's available online."

Aunt Kelly looked ready to protest, but my sister interrupted her.

"You can come see *Pony Pets* with me!" Grace shouted happily.

I didn't really want to go to the movies at all, but even *Pony Pets* would be better than sitting around the house for the rest of the night. I looked out the window and was surprised to see that the rain had stopped.

"Hey, look at that," I said as the clouds parted. "Looks like we might be able to go to Fall Fright after all."

"Why don't you three head upstairs to get ready to go out," Mom told us, "and Kelly and I will do the dishes."

Grace, Ryan, and I wasted little time leaving the kitchen. Dishes were usually my job and if I had the chance to get out of doing them I took it. But halfway up the stairs I remembered I'd left my phone in the basket. Grace had already disappeared into her room, and I told Ryan to go ahead without me.

I returned downstairs but stopped just outside the kitchen in the hall. Mom and Aunt Kelly were talking quietly and something my aunt said caught my attention—they were talking about me. And Dad. "He's changed, but can you blame him?" she said. "No boy his age should lose his father."

"What about Ryan and Reggie?" Mom said.

"My son hasn't exactly lost his father, has he? And most days I think Ryan's better off without Reggie around anyway, sad as that is to say. Ryan's tough."

"I wish Darius was a little tougher," Mom said, and her words felt like tiny little needle pricks in my heart. "He's barely left the house since November. He comes straight home after school, and his friends stopped coming around here a few months ago."

"It'll take time. It's only been ten months."

Mom sighed. "I know. I just worry about him. What if this is it? What if he...?" Whatever Mom was about to say next was cut off by the sound of her crying.

I left my phone in the basket and went upstairs.

CHAPTER 4

THERE WAS A CHILL IN the air as we drove north on Highway 97 from Kelowna to Wight Farm near Ellison Lake. We passed the movie theater, the local college, and then the airport. The farm was just a little farther ahead.

"Move over," Grace complained. She was sandwiched between me and Ryan in the back seat. All three of us were drinking Slushees from the corner store near our house—Mom had bought them for us as a treat since we were splitting up for the night. Only I'd opted to get a jumbo, which was the size of a small bucket. Mom was driving, and Aunt Kelly was riding shotgun.

"For the millionth time, I'm over as far as I can go," I said.

"Quit elbowing me."

"I'm not! I haven't touched you this entire trip!"

"You both smell like ham sandwiches and armpits," Grace said, her nose wrinkled in disgust. "Boys stink."

Ryan laughed. So did Mom and Aunt Kelly. "You ate the same sandwiches we did," I reminded Grace.

"Yeah, but I don't have smelly armpits."

"Don't worry, Grace," Mom said, looking back at us in the rearview mirror. "We'll get rid of the stinky boys and then you'll have the back seat all to yourself on our way back to the movie theater."

Grace cheered.

"You're pretty excited to see *Pony Pets*," Ryan said with a smile.

She nodded. "Mom said it's a short movie, and Aunt Kelly said we'll probably have time to go for hot chocolate before we pick you up. Right, Aunt Kelly?"

"Sure. Anything for my favorite niece."

Grace was Aunt Kelly's only niece, but I didn't want to burst my sister's bubble.

"You never buy me hot chocolate," Ryan said.

"You're not my favorite niece." Aunt Kelly shrugged her shoulders. "Sorry about your luck."

All the joking during the drive made me forget for a moment where we were headed.

But then we pulled up to Fall Fright.

WELCOME TO FALL FRIGHT

OPEN FRIDAY TO SUNDAY IN SEPTEMBER & OCTOBER

PREPARE TO SCREAM!

The paint on the sign was faded and peeling, and the sign was leaning to the left. It looked like a strong breeze might knock it down at any moment.

I instantly had a terrible feeling. Call it intuition or a premonition or a sixth sense, but whatever it was, it was *real*—we had to turn around that instant. Instead Mom pulled into the parking lot—a large grass field turned into a giant mud pit thanks to the day's rainfall—and killed the ignition.

I figured the terrible feeling was probably just me thinking about my dad, and all the times we'd come here. I missed him so much, but now that I'd gotten over my resistance to going to Fall Fright, I knew he'd want me to keep on doing the things we used to do together.

I took in my surroundings. Things seemed a little odd. The parking lot was less than half full but it was only 6:45 p.m. The Scare Staff would just be starting to fill the farm's attractions. Maybe the storm had kept a lot of people away.

"I'm not trying to rain on anyone's parade,"

Aunt Kelly said. She paused, looked at the wet world outside her window, considered what she'd just said, laughed briefly, then continued, "but this place looks like it's gone downhill."

"The offer to come to the movies with us instead is still on the table," Mom added.

Grace perked up. "Yeah! Come to *Pony Pets*!"

I looked at Ryan. He looked back at me like he was wondering if I wanted to bail.

I shook my head and said, "Nah, that's okay. After being stuck inside all day, it will be nice to be outside for a bit."

"All right," Mom said. "We'll meet you back here at ten o'clock. Give me a call if you want me to come pick you up early, okay?"

"Okay," I said, then slapped my forehead. "I left my phone back at home." In the kitchen, where I'd overheard my mom and aunt talking about me, a memory I was trying to forget. I hated people being concerned about me. I hated people treating me like I was a little kid. Was it so weird that I needed some time to get over my dad dying? I was able to return to Fall Fright, wasn't I?

"Don't worry, Dare," Ryan said. "I've got mine."

"Good," Mom said. "And remember: keep to the left."

"Keep to the left?" I had no idea what she was talking about.

"In the maze. I read an article about it. If you keep your left hand on the left wall, you'll eventually get out without becoming turned around and disoriented. It kind of takes all the fun out of mazes, but it works." My skepticism must have been plainly written on my face, because she added with conviction, "Google it."

"Okay, I believe you," I said with a laugh, then thanked her, took the last sip of my Slushee, said quick goodbyes to Grace and Aunt Kelly, and hopped out of the car. Ryan got out the other side, and we walked through the parking lot.

Mud squished loudly underfoot, and we had to step carefully around puddles that had formed in tire ruts.

We walked toward the booth, passing a family with their three young children. The parents did not look happy, and all three kids were on the verge of tears.

"Did they think that was funny?" the dad said.

"If they did, it's a sick joke," the mom agreed.

"You know what I'm going to do? I'm going to write an angry letter."

As she said "write an angry letter," the dad mouthed the words with her. He'd obviously heard this threat from his wife before.

"I'm serious," she said. "Handwritten. And with stern language."

They walked to their car and continued grumbling as they helped their kids into their seats.

"What do you think that was about?" I asked Ryan.

"No idea," he said. "But remind me to never upset that family."

"Yeah," I said, smiling. "I don't think you could handle the stern language they'd sling at you in a letter. Handwritten, no less."

We reached the ticket booth, a small wooden box similar to something you'd see at a really old movie theater, but it had been constructed to look like a coffin. There was a sign on the window that listed admission prices and operating hours, but the booth was empty.

"Hello?" I called. No one answered.

"Hey, look at that." Ryan pointed at a black bell with a skull and crossbones printed on it that sat on the wooden ledge beneath the window. Next to the bell was a small handwritten note that said, PLEASE RING FOR in red lettering, but whoever had written the note hadn't completed the sentence.

"Ring it," I said.

"No way! You ring it."

"C'mon. Ring it."

"I'll ring *you*."

"All right, I'll do it. Chicken." I raised my hand and moved it slowly toward the bell.

"Wait!" Ryan shouted.

I yanked my hand back as the blood drained from my face. "What?!"

He took a step back, pulled his phone out of his pocket, and pointed it at me. "I want to record this." He pressed a few buttons on the screen. "Okay. Go ahead."

"Jerk," I said. I raised my hand again and moved it into the booth with only the slightest moment of hesitation, chiding myself for allowing him to freak me out.

I quickly pressed the bell before I could freak out again. Knowing the bell was some sort of joke prop, I had expected to receive a slight shock or hear an earsplitting sound effect, but neither of those things happened.

Instead, a shrill *ding* rang out, just like one of those metal bells you see on the counter of a hotel.

I looked at Ryan, still filming me on his phone, and shrugged.

"I guess there's nobody—"

I didn't finish my sentence. A man with an axe planted squarely in his head slammed against the inside of the ticket booth window.

"Help me," he moaned.

CHAPTER 5

I TENSED UP AT THE sight of the bloody man, but held my ground and managed not to scream. Ryan, on the other hand, yelled in shock and grabbed my arm so tight that it hurt.

The man with the axe in his head slipped to the floor of the booth, his hands and face leaving a bloody smear on the glass. There was a loud thud and then a door on the side of the booth flew open and he tumbled out. His mouth was open in a silent scream, and his glassy eyes stared blankly up toward the sky.

I took a step toward his body.

"What are you doing?" Ryan hissed from behind.

"He's one of the Scare Staff," I said. "It's an act. He's fine."

Ryan laughed, a nervous and embarrassed sound. "Right. Of course. I knew that."

I glanced at the body, then back at Ryan.

"That's some realistic blood oozing out of his head. Maybe..." I knelt beside the man. He hadn't moved a muscle since he fell to the ground.

"Maybe what?" Ryan asked.

"Maybe there's an axe murderer on the loose. Maybe this dude's really dead."

I placed two fingers on his blood-soaked neck to check for a pulse, the way I'd seen people do it in the movies.

The "dead" man roared and jumped to his feet. I staggered backward, more startled than scared.

"Run for your life!" Ryan screamed.

But before Ryan ran away, the man's roar turned into a full-bodied laugh. "You should've seen the looks on your faces! Well, his face anyway," he said, pointing at my cousin. "Run for your life!" He fell back into a laughing fit and doubled over, holding his side as if he were in pain. "Classic," he added, wiping away tears from the corner of each eye.

"You think it's funny scaring customers?" Ryan shouted, his shoulders tense and his fingers curled into fists.

"Well, yeah," the man said. "Hilarious, actually. And besides, that's what you're here for, isn't it? To be scared?"

He had a point; we *had* come to be scared. "Sure, but usually the scares take place in there." I pointed past the booth in the general direction of the corn maze. "Not before we've bought a ticket."

The man shrugged, a crooked smile on his face. "New policy this year: we're kinda on our own to do as we please. And we're not big on cheap scares." The man stepped back into the booth and closed the door. "Listen, do you want to buy a ticket or not? That first scare was free, but you gotta pay for the rest."

"You all right?" I asked Ryan.

"Yeah, I'm fine," he replied.

I read the admission prices on the window and groaned. "No cheap scares is right," I said, handing over a small stack of cash. The man gave me two tickets.

"Have fun, boys. And prepare...*to scream*!" He steepled his fingers together, threw his axe-impaled head backward, and uttered a deep, exaggerated laugh. "Mwua-ha-ha!"

"C'mon, let's go," I said as I steered Ryan away from the ticket booth.

"Weirdo," Ryan muttered over his shoulder.

"And proud of it," the man said with a tip of an imaginary hat.

We walked into the farmyard where we

could have a good look at all of the attractions. The property was partially lit by two dozen or so light poles, but nearly half of the bulbs were burned out or flickering sporadically. Behind the entrance and ticket booth was an apple orchard and a rusty tractor with a trailer hitched to it for wagon rides to and from the pumpkin patch. Beside the orchard was an old red barn that had been turned into a creepy petting zoo for younger kids, and beside that was the Wights' farmhouse. The sight of that house always made me feel a little uncomfortable. It was a two-story home with dirty walls and shuttered windows, surrounded by a grove of black, gnarled trees.

Past the farmhouse and the barn was Fall Fright's main attraction—the corn maze. I could see an old combine harvester parked beyond the maze, its sharp blades gleaming in the moonlight. The maze's entrance was cut into a wall of cornstalks seven feet tall. There was a scarecrow holding a large scythe standing to the right of the entrance. The scythe's blade was positioned above the entrance, just like in the TV commercial.

"It doesn't look like they've changed a thing since last year," I said.

"So?" Ryan asked.

"They usually change things up each year," I said. "You know, to keep things fresh."

"That skull bell and the axe guy were new, right?"

"Yeah, that's true."

There were a few people seated in the wagon attached to the tractor, waiting for the ride to start. I could see others walking between the attractions, but it definitely wasn't as busy as it had been any other year.

"So, what do you want to do first?" I asked, trying to sound positive. "Are you ready to brave the petting zoo?"

Ryan smiled for the first time since Axe Head had scared the pants off him.

"Maybe we should work our way up to that," he

joked. "Besides, the corn maze is the main attraction, right? Why don't we start there? And if it's any good, we'll still have time to go through it a second time."

"Cool," I said, and led the way.

We stopped at the entrance to the maze and looked up at the scarecrow with the scythe. His pumpkin face glared down at us with a jagged smile. The pumpkin was rotting and had been pecked at by birds.

A few kids stepped around us and walked through the entrance, disappearing inside.

Ryan took a step forward, but I stopped him by placing my hand on his shoulder. He looked back at me in confusion.

I pointed up at the blade above him. "Watch your head," I said.

"Ha, ha," he said with a roll of his eyes. "Very funny."

"You should listen to your friend," a gruff voice said from behind us.

I hadn't heard anyone approach, but I turned around and saw an old man with a face more wrinkled than a raisin staring at us with beady eyes. He had long stringy hair that spilled out from under the straw hat he wore. Old Man Wight wrung his bony hands together as if strangling an imaginary neck.

"You wouldn't be the first kids to die in that maze," he said.

CHAPTER 6

THE OLD MAN DESCENDED INTO a hacking, sputtering coughing fit. He yanked a yellow-stained handkerchief out of the breast pocket of his shirt and covered his mouth with it. He coughed loudly into the handkerchief before stuffing it back into his pocket. One dirty corner of it poked out. I tried my best not to look directly at it.

"What did you say?" I asked.

His bushy eyebrows narrowed as he eyed me up and down, silently judging me.

"You heard me," he said. He removed his straw hat and rubbed the top of his head with his handkerchief. I closed my eyes and shuddered.

"You think just because you own the place you can scare us?" I said. I didn't believe for a second that any kids had actually died at Fall Fright.

That seemed to take him aback. "You know who I am?" he grumbled.

I nodded. "Well, yeah."

"Where are my manners?" he said suddenly. He cleared his throat and extended his hand. I shook it. "The name's Edgar Wight."

"I'm Darius," I said, a little surprised by his sudden change in demeanor, "and this is my cousin Ryan."

"Cousin, eh?" Mr. Wight's face fell. He looked like I'd just told him his dog died or, I don't know, his pig or his rooster or his cow—whatever farmers consider pets. "Isn't that nice, you two being cousins *and* friends. Don't take that for granted."

"Okay," I said, thinking that was a weird thing for him to say.

Another group of kids walked between us and into the maze, which seemed to snap Wight out of someplace his mind had taken him. He blinked a few times and shook his head, then looked from me to Ryan. "I'm sorry if I startled you earlier. I haven't been myself lately. I haven't been myself in...some time. What am I saying?" He laughed nervously. "You boys came here to be scared, but not like this. I hope you enjoy the corn maze. It's very special to me. Or at least, it used to be."

He took one last look at the maze and then turned and stalked off before I could say anything else.

Once Wight was out of earshot, Ryan said, "I don't think he gets out much."

I laughed. "Yeah. I think he could use a vacation."

Ryan turned to enter the maze.

"Hang on," I said, stopping him. "That Slushee I drank on the way here was huge and I don't want to get stuck in there before I do something about it. Mind if I run to the bathroom?"

"Be my guest," Ryan said. "I'll wait here."

I scanned our surroundings but didn't see a porta potty anywhere nearby.

Ryan picked up on my mild distress and said, "Just go behind the house."

"Wight's house?"

"Sure, why not?"

"I don't know. I just met him. It feels too soon to pee on his house."

Ryan didn't answer but sighed and rolled his eyes like he thought I was being ridiculous. "Then walk a little farther and go on his barn. Would that make you more comfortable, Your Highness?"

I nodded. "As a matter of fact, yeah, it would." I didn't want to give Ryan an opportunity to tease me further, plus my bladder was starting to really hurt, so I hustled around the barn, hoping no one had seen me sneak back there.

Feeling much better, I took my time walking back the way I had come past Wight's house. There was no rush. Not anymore.

Something caught my eye as I strolled between the house and the trees. Something unusual.

Staring out from a tangle of overgrown weeds were the empty eye sockets of a human skull.

CHAPTER 7

GET A GRIP, DARIUS, I thought. *It's not a skull. It's just a rock.*

It was about the same size as a skull, and it did have two round indents roughly where eye sockets would be. But other than that, it didn't resemble a human skull at all. I figured I must be extra jittery thanks to the couple of scares I'd already had, plus the memories of my dad that had been on my mind.

The two indents seemed to follow me—not

unlike eyes in a painting—as I bent down to examine the rock a little more closely. It was covered in dirt and something reddish brown. Bloodstains?

Suddenly the skull began to shake and something like a thin, pink snake poked out from behind it. A small brown blur bounded over the rock and lunged straight for me.

I jumped back in shock before realizing the brown blur was a mouse. The pink snake had been its tail, and it hadn't lunged straight for me but had leapt to the ground and then scampered off and slipped into a hole in the wall of the house.

"You got me, mouse," I said.

I turned to rejoin Ryan, but then I had an idea.

～ⁿᵒ🌀ᵒ〜

"What took you so long?" Ryan asked when I returned to the entrance of the maze. "You didn't drink *that* much Slushee."

I painted my face with a pained expression and groaned in discomfort.

"You okay, Dare?" Ryan said. "You don't look so hot."

"I don't *feel* so hot," I said. My hands held my gut as if I was suffering from severe cramps. In reality, I was holding the concealed rock beneath my sweater, hoping Ryan wouldn't notice the bulge beneath my hands. "I think it was something I ate."

"Oh, no," Ryan said. "We ate the same stuff. I don't want whatever you've got."

"Thanks," I said sarcastically, momentarily breaking character, a mistake I quickly covered up by groaning again.

"Do you need me to call your mom to come get us?"

"I think..." I said. I looked at a point in the distance over Ryan's shoulder and straightened a little as my eyes widened and my mouth fell open.

"What's that behind you?"

"What?" Ryan asked in a panic. He spun around and looked from left to right.

I pulled the rock out of my sweater and placed it on top of my head. I yanked my jacket up, concealing my head within it, and put it up on top of the rock, hoping that would hold it in place. I didn't need to pin the rock between my head and the jacket for long, just long enough for Ryan to turn back around.

I raised my hands menacingly and waited. I didn't wait long.

Ryan's scream was loud and piercing. He sounded like a character in a horror movie who was about to meet a particularly nasty end.

My laughter was as genuine as my cousin's scream but not nearly as loud. I continued to laugh as I grabbed the rock and pushed my head back up through my sweater.

"You jerk!" Ryan said. He ripped the rock out of my hands.

"I got you," I said. "I got you good."

"Well, yeah. I'm expecting scares from the people who work here, not from you." He looked at the rock in his hands and wrinkled his nose in disgust. "I can't believe I thought this thing was a skull."

"Don't let it bother you too much," I said. "I thought it was a skull, too. I found it behind the farmhouse." I held out my hand to take it back.

"No way," Ryan said, pulling the rock closer to his chest. "It's mine now. I don't know how yet, but I'm going to get you back."

"Good luck," I said encouragingly. "While you're trying to come up with something, want to head into the maze? Or are you feeling too chicken?"

Ryan scoffed. "Don't worry about me. Worry about yourself."

"Thanks for the pro tip," I said. "After you." I gestured to the entrance.

We walked into the corn maze and almost immediately came to a fork in the path and our first decision: turn left or right. Nothing unusual could be seen in either direction, so I turned right.

"Where do you think you're going?" Ryan asked incredulously.

"Uh, this way?"

"But that's a right turn."

"So?"

"Your mom said to keep to the left."

"No. She said to keep a hand on the left wall. There's a difference. Besides, that takes all the fun out of it," I countered. "Let's just wander for a bit and see what happens." Ryan didn't look sold, so I added, "If we don't get out in, I don't know, fifteen minutes, we can try my mom's technique, okay?"

"Fine," he said. He looked like a kid who'd just been told he had to finish all his broccoli before he could leave the kitchen table.

I could hear footsteps somewhere in the distance. But as far as I could see, it was just me and Ryan.

"So, how do you like your new home?" I asked as we walked.

"When we first moved there, I didn't love it as much as I thought I would," Ryan said. "But it's grown on me. There's lots to do, and it's pretty sweet being by the ocean. Mom's taken me to a couple of hockey games."

"That's really cool."

Ryan stopped walking and nodded. "You gotta come visit soon. You'd love it."

"I'd like to," I said, wondering why we'd stopped.

"It might help you—I don't know—get your mind off things."

I sighed and walked on. "Not you, too." Ryan followed as I turned a corner.

"What's the matter?" he asked.

"Everyone's been telling me I need to move on with my life. First it was Mom, then it was some kids at school and a teacher or two, and then, earlier this afternoon, it was your mom, too."

"Hey, man. I didn't say anything about moving on with your life."

"No, but you did say I should get my mind off things," I said. "And I have a really good bet I know exactly what *thing* you're talking about."

"Well, sure. I don't think it would kill you to come visit me for a couple of days and have a good time."

"And I want to," I said with a sigh. "It sounds awesome. I'm just tired of people telling me how I should feel about my dad, that's all."

"I get that," Ryan said. "I'm sorry. I won't say anything else, but I do hope you come soon."

"Thanks," I said. "And I'm sorry, too."

"What for?"

I smiled. "For scaring you with that dumb rock. I didn't think it would get you that good."

"It didn't get me *that* good." Ryan gave me a playful shove. I shot him a doubtful look. "Okay, it got me."

"I think city life is making you soft."

We turned another corner without pausing to think where we were headed, and an imposing figure—eight or nine feet tall—blocked our path. He wore a dark cloak, and his skin appeared to be peeling off his face. The monster lunged for us as soon as we locked eyes.

CHAPTER 8

RYAN YELLED AND NEARLY LOST his grip on the rock. I tensed up and stopped breathing for a moment but managed, for the most part, to keep cool.

The man's skin wasn't peeling off his face; he had a scarecrow face. More accurately, he wore a scarecrow mask. We'd been shocked by a member of the Scare Staff.

Ryan and I laughed, patted each other's shoulders, and wound our way around the scarecrow. He glared down at us as we passed and followed close at our heels, groaning and muttering as we walked away. Both his height and the somewhat jerky way he moved made it clear he had stilts concealed beneath his ragged pants.

"That was pretty cool," Ryan admitted once we'd turned a corner. "He actually scared me."

"As much as the rock?" I asked.

"Let's just drop the rock, okay?"

"You first," I retorted. "Why not toss it?"

"No, no, no. I'm hanging on to it a little longer. I'm going to get you somehow, remember?"

"How could I forget?" I laughed. "But I think I was all scared out before we even entered the maze."

"Old Man Wight?"

"Yeah, and his warning that we wouldn't be the first kids to die in this maze."

Ryan nodded. "That was creepy. What do you think he meant by that?"

"Who knows? He's super weird—why is he so obsessed with this maze? It's cool, but it's just a bunch of paths and dead ends cut through cornstalks."

"It was almost like he had two personalities, like Jekyll and Hyde or something," Ryan said.

Wher, wher, wher!

It was the revving of a chainsaw, and it sounded close. Not right-behind-me close, but maybe on-the-other-side-of-that-hedge close—or worse, just-around-the-corner close.

In other words, *too* close.

Wait a minute, slow down, I thought. *It's not real.* For a minute I'd forgotten where we were, and that all of the scares were manufactured. The chainsaw would be operated by a member of the Scare Staff, and the sharp chain would be removed from it for safety.

Still, I never enjoyed being chased by a sixteen- or seventeen-year-old with a heavy power tool, chain or no chain.

A kid who looked only slightly older than us jumped out from around a corner, raised his chainsaw high in the air above his head, and then ran straight at us.

Ryan and I yelled and laughed at the same time and sprinted away from the Scare Staffer. We took a few turns left and a couple of turns right until the sound of the chainsaw faded away.

We laughed some more, and I noticed his hands were empty.

"Hey, where's the rock?" I asked.

"I dropped it back there."

"Do you want to go back for it?"

"Nah, I was getting bored of carrying it around, and I wasn't actually going to try to scare you with it."

I eyed him suspiciously, trying to figure out if he was lying. "Are you just saying that so I'll drop my guard?"

"No, man. I swear. I dropped it by accident."

Ryan looked around and added, "Which way now?"

I shook my head as I caught my breath.

"Don't know. I'm completely turned around."
I looked up at the sky. "I think it's possible to get a directional bearing based on the position of the stars."

"Can you do that?"

"Nah, never tried it," I said. "But I saw it in a movie once. *Camp Chaos*. A troop of Boy Scouts got lost on an island and were being chased by a wild person with some deadly disease."

"Did the Boy Scouts survive?"

"Most of them died. In fact, I don't think any of them made it to the end credits."

Ryan sighed. "I don't know why I asked." He took another look around and took the second path on our right.

"Hey, where are you headed?" I asked while following him. "Did you see something down that way?"

"No," he replied over his shoulder. "But it's better than just standing around going nowhere."

I couldn't argue with that, and I didn't have

any other options, so I decided to let my cousin take the lead for a while.

We made many turns and walked down countless corridors, listening to the creaks of cornstalks bending with the breeze. We didn't pass another soul, neither Scare Staff nor customer, which struck me as odd. The night grew a little older and a lot colder. We pressed on.

Just as I was beginning to get anxious, Ryan spotted something.

"What's that?" he asked, pointing at the path ahead.

There was a small gray shape on the ground. We raced toward it. I figured out what it was a moment before Ryan.

"It's the rock," he said, bending to pick it up. "We've been going in circles."

My stomach dropped. "We're lost."

CHAPTER 9

AS UNSETTLING AS IT FELT to be lost, I actually felt worse than that. A whole lot worse.

When I saw the rock with the two indents that looked a little like eyes I was overcome with an unshakable conviction that something was watching us. Worse than that: not only was something watching us, but it didn't want us to leave.

I shook my head. That thought didn't make sense, at least in any rational way. But still, the thought persisted.

Something watching doesn't want us to leave.

I felt eyes on the back of my neck and spun around but didn't see anyone other than my cousin. And yet the feeling didn't go away.

"I have this weird feeling," I said slowly, "that something is trying to keep us here."

"In the maze?" Ryan asked.

I nodded, unsure what else I could say without sounding completely nuts.

"Let's put your theory to the test," Ryan said. He left the rock on the ground and stood up. "Let's stick to the left wall—like your mom said—and get out of here, no matter how long it takes. If we leave the rock here, we'll know if we pass through this same spot again, which we shouldn't, I don't think. I don't know."

No, you didn't. Not in Wight's maze. "All right, let's go. The sooner we get out of here the better."

Ryan nodded and took the first turn on our left. I caught up and walked on his right, every now and again falling behind him when the path narrowed and the cornstalks closed in on us. We hardly spoke for the next five or ten minutes. (Or was it fifteen? Twenty? It was hard to keep track of time.) In all that time we still didn't pass a single member of the Scare Staff or another group of people trying to find their own way out. It was as if we had accidentally entered a section of the maze that was off-limits, a place where we shouldn't have been. A shiver spread up my spine.

I kept my eyes on the left wall, not exactly sure which direction we were headed, but certain we were moving farther away from the spot where we'd begun my mom's tactic.

But then we turned a corner and I saw something in the dirt up ahead. Although I couldn't see it in detail I knew exactly what it was.

"Is that...? Is that the same rock?" Ryan asked.

"It is," I said, unable to keep the despair out of my voice.

"But we stuck to the left."

"All right, look," I said. "It's possible sticking to the left wall, in this corner of the maze, somehow always leads back to this spot. So let's try sticking to the right wall. That will get us out, guaranteed."

Ryan nodded, but he looked defeated.

"C'mon," I said encouragingly. "I'll lead this time."

He followed without a word.

Right, right, left, left, right. I kept track of the turns, creating a mental map in my mind. Left, right, left. We were definitely heading away from the rock. I felt like a lab rat in search of a piece of cheese while scientists loomed overhead, tracking our progress and writing observations on clipboards. I hated that feeling, like I wasn't in control of my own actions, of my own destiny. Right, left. But it didn't matter how I felt. I was getting us out of the maze, I was sure of that.

Right.

We turned one more corner and nearly stepped on the rock.

"You've got to be kidding me," Ryan said.

"I don't understand," I said.

"What the—"

"Impossible."

Ryan picked up the rock and whipped it over the cornstalk wall to our left. It sailed out of sight, and I heard it hit the ground in the distance with a thud.

"You could've hit someone," I said.

"I don't care!" Ryan wailed. "I just want out of here."

We really *were* trapped in the maze. There was no other explanation. We'd gone left and we'd gone right, and both paths led us straight back here, straight back to this area where no one else was. We were lost and we were alone.

I spun around, suddenly feeling eyes on the back of my neck again. Like before, there was no one there. Just us and the corn.

But that didn't explain the feeling in the pit of my stomach. The feeling that we were being watched, that we'd been watched ever since we stumbled into this part of the maze. The feeling that we were in really big trouble.

"What now?" Ryan asked.

"I don't know," I said helplessly.

"I've got an idea," Ryan said suddenly. He locked eyes with me and nodded. "I'm following the rock." Before I could ask him what he meant, he showed me, charging through the wall of corn on the left, the same one he'd thrown the rock over.

For a moment I stood alone, a little dumbfounded. It actually wasn't a bad idea. If the paths wouldn't lead us out, we'd make our own path.

I followed Ryan, feeling more in control than I'd felt for a while. It felt good.

"Wait up!" I called out. I couldn't see him, but it wasn't hard to figure out where he'd gone. The cornstalks were damaged and bent where he'd run through them.

I stumbled into an opening and finally caught

up to Ryan. He was sprawled out on his back in the dirt, holding his hands to his head. And his attacker, a tall, dark figure, was leering over him, ready to strike again.

CHAPTER 10

"RYAN!" I YELLED, RUNNING TO his side. "Hey, you all right?" I asked, bending over him where he lay.

He pushed himself up onto his hands and knees, then shakily got to his feet. "Yeah, sure, I'm fine," he said, sounding more embarrassed than anything else. "I didn't see our friend here until I ran straight into him." He hooked a thumb at his attacker.

I turned around to look at the creature and noticed he didn't have a head. The attacker was, I realized, a scarecrow. His pumpkin head was split open on the ground a yard or so from the post that held him up. And a few yards past the broken head was the rock, half-buried in the ground where it had landed.

"Well," I said, "I'm glad that's his head cracked open in the dirt and not yours."

"You and me both."

I picked up a piece of the pumpkin's face, one triangle eye and half a jagged grin. It reminded me of the scarecrow guarding the entrance to the maze, except this pumpkin wasn't rotting. It looked freshly carved. I dropped the piece back to the ground and looked at the scarecrow's body. It wore a long black trench coat that billowed open in the wind, revealing a tangle of tree branches beneath. It looked like the scarecrow's torso was made of gnarled roots that had been ripped out of the dirt and dressed like a man. He had no legs, only arms. Bunches of branches jutted out of both sleeves like long, wooden tentacles that passed for fingers. Looking at the scarecrow made my skin crawl.

But the scarecrow wasn't the only thing that was off-putting. There was something else nagging at me, something I couldn't quite put my finger on. Ryan felt it, too. "Everything about this place feels really weird, stranger than the rest of the maze," he said. "And that's saying something."

"Yeah, I know."

I peered through misty clouds of my own breath, which also didn't make sense—it was cold, but not that cold—and looked around. And it dawned on me what was so unsettling.

There were no cleared paths, nothing leading into or out of this clearing we'd stumbled upon. I walked in a quick circle and checked the walls, just to be sure.

Ryan picked up on what was bothering me. "Why is there...an empty circular room in the middle of the maze?"

"But it's not empty, is it?" I said, pointing at the scarecrow. "And that makes it even stranger. Why would Old Man Wight go to the trouble of clearing this area and putting a Halloween decoration here if no one was ever going to see it?" A shiver racked my body and I inhaled quickly. "Man, did it get cold fast or what?"

Ryan nodded and blew on his hands. "We should move on. Get the blood pumping."

"Sounds good," I said. I walked through the wall of corn opposite the spot we'd entered, figuring it made sense to carry on in the way we'd been headed before Ryan had run into the scarecrow. But after nine or ten steps I realized Ryan hadn't followed.

"Ryan?" I called. He didn't answer.

"Ryan!" I said a little louder.

"Darius."

It was Dad. Not Ryan.

Dad.

He was standing in the wall of corn beside me,

surrounded by absolute darkness. And then, in the blink of an eye, he was gone.

I closed my eyes and rubbed my face. I heard someone approach. I opened my eyes again but only saw my cousin. I looked left and right and felt my heart hammer against my ribs like a fist trying to punch a hole through my chest, but Dad was still nowhere to be seen.

Get a grip, I thought. *He was never here to begin with. You're seeing things.*

"You okay?" Ryan asked. "You look like someone who's run into a wooden post."

"I'm fine. I thought I saw..." I trailed off and shook my head. What had I thought I'd seen? I shrugged. "Nothing. I didn't see anything."

"You sure?" Ryan asked, looking at me skeptically.

"Yeah, I'm sure. C'mon." I pushed through the corn. "What took you so long to catch up?"

"I wanted to replace the scarecrow's head with the rock." Ryan laughed lightly. "I felt guilty for decapitating him. But I got a shock when I placed it on his neck and it fell off. I didn't bother trying again."

I frowned. "You can't get a shock from a rock."

"Tell that to the rock that just shocked me."

I shrugged. It wasn't worth arguing the point.

Before long we broke through into another path. "Think we should go this way or that?" I asked, pointing first down one direction of the path and then the other.

"Neither," he said. "Let's keep cutting through walls so we..." Ryan trailed off.

After not seeing or even hearing another person for what felt like a long time, we were no longer alone. A boy no more than nine or ten years old, ashen-faced and unblinking, had appeared as if out of thin air.

"Help me," he said in a hoarse whisper.

"What's wrong?" Ryan asked.

"Help me," the boy repeated.

"Where are your parents?" I asked. I had a

feeling the boy was lost...kind of like us, but too young. He shouldn't be alone. I took a step toward him.

He took a step back in response. "Help me," he said again.

Ryan raised his hands to the boy in the universal show of "I'm not a threat."

"How can we help you?" he asked.

"You have to protect me," the boy said, his tone full of fear and stone-cold serious. "You have to protect me from the bad man. He's coming, coming for us all...and it's your fault."

CHAPTER 11

RYAN LOOKED AT ME WITH concern and then turned back to the boy. "Who's the bad man? What does he want with us? How is that our fault?"

The boy shook his head, took another step backward, and looked from side to side. "I've said too much. He'll be here soon, and he'll be mad if he catches me talking to you. I have to go. I have to hide."

"Wait!" Ryan said. "You said you needed our help."

"I was wrong. You can't help me," the boy said. "Now that he's coming, you can't even help yourselves." He spun around and sprinted silently away from us. He ran into the corn and disappeared.

"Well, that was weird," Ryan said.

I laughed. "He was part of the Scare Staff."

"What? You're kidding, right?"

"Nope."

"But he was so young."

I opened my mouth to offer a logical explanation, but found I couldn't think of one. "He was young."

"And his costume looked so real. He was so pale."

"Yeah, he was."

"And he was super scared! I mean, his fear was so real it rubbed off on me."

"Me too, just a little," I admitted. "He was one of the most convincing actors I've ever seen here, any year I've come. But he was still an actor."

Ryan didn't look convinced, so I added,

"Watch. Any minute now some dude with a hook for a hand or dressed like a clown or wearing a skeleton mask—you know, the bad man that kid mentioned—is going to jump out from his hiding place and yell and scream. It's a classic horror movie technique. A little bit of foreshadowing that makes the inevitable scare even scarier."

We waited and watched. A minute passed, then another and another. No bad man jumped out and yelled at us.

"Maybe he's on his coffee break," I offered weakly, "and forgot to tell the kid."

"Don't you need to be, like, fifteen years old to have a job?"

"Maybe he looks younger than he is. Or maybe he's being paid under the table."

"Yeah, maybe, I guess," Ryan said.

I wasn't sure if I had managed to convince my cousin that the boy worked there, but the more I thought about it the more I grew concerned that the boy *hadn't* been part of the Scare Staff.

"Now I'm worried there's a kid who's actually lost in this maze, like us," I said. "But unlike us, he's all alone."

"And also being chased by a bad man. Don't forget about that," Ryan added. "If that's the case, what do we do?"

"There's not much we *can* do. Keep our eyes open for him, I guess, and tell an adult once we get out of here. Maybe we'll find his parents at the exit."

"Maybe I should call someone." Ryan turned on his phone and tapped a few times on the screen.

"Who are you going to call?" I asked. "The police?"

He shook his head and returned his phone to his pocket. "I can't even get a signal."

"That's weird. We're not *that* far out in the country."

"Think this corn is blocking the signal? It's pretty tall."

"Maybe," I said, not believing for a second

that the corn was blocking his phone. "Let's keep on cutting through in the same direction until we get out of here, and then I'll use your phone to call my mom."

I wished, not for the first time, that my dad was with us. He'd know what to do. He'd take over, help the lost kid, and get us out of the maze, no problem. In his absence, those responsibilities had fallen to Ryan and me. The thought of Dad suddenly took me back to what had happened ten months ago.

My parents, Grace, and I had been on a hike. We'd found a nice, secluded area beside a stream for a break. There was a large rock that looked like a bench. My dad had stopped, clutched at his chest, and...

I stopped picturing it, those final, terrible moments spent with my father.

I took a deep breath to clear my mind and said, "This way, then." I reached into the darkness of the corn and bent one of the stalks to create an opening.

Something grabbed my hand.

I couldn't move. My entire body had seized up. I couldn't even yell out in shock or pain. And the pain... The pain was like nothing I'd ever felt before.

My hand was as cold as if it had been dunked in a vat of ice water. But it burned, too, hot and electrical. The excruciating sensation snaked quickly up my arm and spread through my chest. It felt like my bones were freezing while my skin was melting, and every beat of my heart threatened to crack my body in half.

"Darius?" Ryan said in panic. "What's wrong?"

I couldn't respond, but I could hear him. There was nothing wrong with my ears, and there was nothing wrong with my eyes. I could see just fine. And I saw, finally, who had grabbed my hand.

Without releasing his grasp on my hand, someone stepped out from the wall of corn and

I knew at once (my brain was working just fine) that it was the person the boy had warned us about...

The bad man.

CHAPTER 12

FROM MY ANGLE LOOKING UP at him, he appeared to be nearly as tall as the cornstalks he'd just pushed through. He had to be at least six feet tall, if not taller, and he had reddish-brown hair down to his shoulders. He had a chest like a barrel and arms thick and rough with muscle. He wore dirty overalls and a red flannel shirt with the sleeves rolled up to his elbows.

I noticed all of that in a flash—since I still couldn't move. I could do nothing but stand and stare at him. He was no Scare Staffer, no actor—I knew that without a shadow of a doubt.

I didn't have the ability or the time to ponder it any further as the pain had reached new heights. My head throbbed, my insides churned, and my vision dimmed. *This is it*, I thought. *This is the end. I'm going to die in Old Man Wight's maze with my cousin forced to stand by and watch helplessly.*

"This is the only thing I like about being dead," the bad man said in a deep voice that boomed inside my skull. "All I have to do is touch you, and you're utterly helpless."

"Let him go," I heard Ryan say from somewhere beside me. His voice sounded like it was far away and underwater. I couldn't turn my head to look.

The bad man laughed. "Or what? You'll stop me? If you touch me you'll end up like him. Want to switch places and give your life for his?"

If Ryan answered I didn't hear him. My heart drummed in my ears.

THUD-thud. THUD-thud. THUD-thud.

It was all I could hear.

THUD-thud. THUD-thud. Thud-thud.

And it was slowing down, growing softer, softer...

Thud-thud...thud-thud...thud-thud...

My eardrums felt like they'd filled with thick fluid, and my sight was whittled down to a pin-prick of light.

Thud...thud...

I stopped breathing.

Thud.

Just when I thought my heart had beaten its final beat, light flooded my vision and sounds came screaming back to life. I sucked in a deep lungful of air. The burning/freezing feeling left my body as if it was being vacuumed out, and I fell backward.

The bad man was no longer holding my hand. He was spinning in mad circles and yelling in anger. The boy! The boy had wrapped his tiny arms around the man's neck, choking him. The man was trying to get the boy off his back.

I felt hands pull me up by the armpits. It was Ryan.

"You okay?" he asked.

"I'm okay," I mumbled. My tongue felt swollen, my bones ached, and my head was foggy, but I was amazed how quickly I was beginning to feel better considering how awful I'd felt while the bad man touched me.

"Good," Ryan said. "Let's get out of here."

"What about him?" I asked, pointing at the boy. He was still clinging desperately to the man's neck as if he was riding the world's angriest bull. I doubted he'd last much longer before the man tossed him aside like a doll.

"Forget about him," Ryan said. "We've got to save ourselves."

I didn't love the idea of leaving the boy to fend for himself after he'd risked his life to save us, but I also couldn't argue with Ryan. What would happen when the man flung the boy aside? What would happen if he grabbed me *and* Ryan at the same time? Who would save us then?

Ryan jumped through the corn and ran, and I followed. The stalks whipped me from both sides. I raised my hands to shield my face but didn't dare slow down. We ran through the maze and cut through paths and I saw something I hadn't seen in a long time: people. Living people. I caught a glimpse of a group of kids, and a few seconds later a man in a werewolf mask howled at us as we crashed out of one wall and through another.

"Hey!" I heard Werewolf bellow after us, his muffled voice fading as we sped away without slowing. "You have to stay on the paths!"

"Wait!" someone else yelled from somewhere close within the corn. Thinking we'd been caught by another Scare Staff member, I glanced over my shoulder to see who'd followed us.

It was the boy.

"Thanks—" I said, amazed he'd escaped, but he cut me off.

"There's no time." He pointed behind me, the direction we'd been heading in before he stopped us; I looked over my shoulder but saw nothing. "Someone's coming."

That's when I noticed the look of fear in his eyes as he stared not at me, but around me, and I had a feeling I knew what—or rather, who—he thought was approaching.

Even still, I had to ask to be sure. "The bad man?"

"The baddest of them all," he responded. Baddest of them all? What did he mean by that?

Heavy footsteps approached quickly from behind. I spun around just as the bad man came crashing through a wall of corn. How did he get ahead of us? I raised my hands defensively in front of my face, knowing that wouldn't do a thing to save me from his death touch, knowing this time I didn't stand a chance.

CHAPTER 13

A MAN BURST INTO VIEW, but it wasn't the bad man. Just a weird old man.

Wight stopped dead in his tracks when he saw Ryan and me. His head bobbed up and down like a chicken pecking at bits of corn, and his wild eyes searched us up and down and then looked past us left and right. He seemed disappointed to see us, or maybe agitated. Probably both.

Baddest of them all, the boy had said before fleeing in terror.

"I heard a voice," Wight said desperately, short of breath and full of nerves. "A voice! Who was here with you?"

"I don't know what you're—" I said but he cut me off.

"Don't play dumb with me," he said, his voice a low growl. "This is my property, and I demand to know who was with you just a moment ago."

"Seriously, old man, back off!" Ryan said, stepping up beside me.

Something inside Wight seemed to snap. His upper lip curled back, revealing the top row of his yellowed, crooked teeth. His mental state appeared to be balanced precariously on a knife-edge. And then, just when I feared he was about to have another angry outburst, his chest heaved a little and he sucked air in quickly through his teeth, as if he'd been stung by a wasp.

"I'm sorry," he said. And then, as if noticing us for the first time, he said, "You're the two boys I spoke with earlier."

I still didn't trust him—not by a long shot—but I was beginning to understand part of the reason he was so weird. He'd been living for years on a haunted farm.

"Yeah, we spoke earlier," I said. "The voice you heard was... Well, we found a boy in the maze, maybe nine or ten years old. He seemed lost. He was about this tall—" I held my hand up to my shoulder, "and he had reddish-blond hair."

Wight removed his hat and twisted it in his fingers. His lower lip quivered and the wrinkles around his eyes deepened. He nodded, unbunched his hat, and set it back on top of his head with a deep sigh. "He's not lost. He's my cousin. His name was Clive. He...he's dead."

"What?" Ryan whispered.

"He's dead?" I said, my brain taking a moment to process that information.

But the more I thought about it, the more it made sense. That's why he looked a little odd and moved without making a sound, and also how he could touch the bad man without it hurting the way it had hurt me.

Assuming Clive and Wight had been about the same age, Clive must've died fifty or sixty years ago.

"How did he die?" I asked quietly, hoping the question didn't set the old man off. He was Jekyll right now—calm and more or less even-tempered. I had no desire to awaken Hyde—angry and quick to fly off the handle.

Wight opened his mouth to answer but then snapped it shut and looked around. He shivered, and his back made a series of sharp cracks and pops. "This is no place for a story like that," he said. "Come back to my house, and I'll tell you."

I nodded, and Wight started to walk away. Ryan and I followed, leaving a bit of distance between us and the old man.

"Smart move," Ryan said in a low voice. "Huh?"

"Letting him lead us out of the maze, then ditching him once we're free."

"No, I'm going to follow him to his house and hear him out."

Ryan shook his head, speechless. We turned a corner.

A large pig-headed man wearing a bloody apron blocked our path. He clanged two butcher knives together and said, "Oink, oink, oink!"

Wight waved his hand without breaking his stride. "Evening, Jerry," he said.

The pig man straightened up and lowered his knives. "Oh, hiya, Mr. Wight." He started to lift the pig mask off his head but noticed Ryan and me for the first time and quickly lowered it back down.

"Hey, Jerry," I said.

Jerry waved and, unsure how to respond, said, "Um...oink, oink?"

"Oink, oink," Ryan responded.

Once we had put enough distance between us and Jerry, Ryan continued. "You can't be seriously considering entering that guy's house."

"I want to know more about Clive," I said.

"Forget Clive! Who cares?"

"I do, and you should, too."

"Why?"

"Because the bad man who tried to kill me is still out there somewhere, and I have a feeling he won't rest until we're dead."

"Let's just go home and forget all about this night," Ryan said. "When our moms pick us up we'll tell them we had an uneventful time and then we'll quickly change the topic to *Pony Pets* and we'll *never speak about this again*." Although he tried to keep his voice down, the last few words came out loudly.

Wight looked back over his shoulder. "You boys still coming?"

"Yes, we're coming," Ryan told Wight and then added quietly to me, "but not into his house. No way."

I pushed on. "What if that ghost follows us home?"

"Aren't ghosts supposed to haunt one place forever or something?"

"Do you want to take that chance? Let's ask to use Wight's phone. While we wait to be picked up, we'll hear him out."

Ryan sighed but he didn't argue so I knew I was beginning to win him over.

"We'll stick together," I continued, trying to strengthen my case. "And besides, he's ancient. Even if he tries anything, we'll overpower him easily."

Although he still didn't look like he loved the idea, he said, "Fine. But if we end up dead, I'm never going to forgive you."

"Fair enough," I said with a smile.

We followed Wight around another corner, and I was overcome with a feeling of relief: the exit was dead ahead. The air smelled a little cleaner and felt a little warmer once we left the maze, and I had to resist the sudden urge to drop to my knees and kiss the ground. Ryan actually exhaled, as if he'd been holding his breath.

But my relief was short-lived. As we approached the Wight farmhouse, the same feeling I'd had when I'd seen it during previous years came back to me. It was a feeling that screamed two words at me: *Stay away!*

Wight held the door open for us, and we stepped inside.

CHAPTER 14

THE FIRST THING THAT CROSSED my mind as soon as I stepped into the front hallway was that I had made a grave mistake.

The air was musty and tinged with rot, as if something dead was hidden in a closet or the cellar or the attic, or maybe the bathroom. It didn't look like any of the furniture had been updated in fifty years. In fact, it didn't look like any of the furniture had been *dusted* in fifty years. The only light was from the moon, a pallid blue haze that cast odd shadows through the dirty windows.

Wight turned on a lamp on the front hall table, but the light didn't do much to cut the gloom and improve my spirits. He waved for us to follow him deeper into his house.

We passed a couple of doors as we walked down the hallway. One of them was open a crack. I peeked in and saw a picture of Clive on a table, surrounded by other stuff.

As soon as we entered the kitchen I was hit with a wall of foul odor thick enough to taste. The sink was filled with dirty dishes, and a garbage can in the corner was overflowing with waste. At least the smell I'd noticed when we first walked in wasn't a dead thing in a closet or the cellar or the attic or the bathroom.

"You boys want a drink?" Wight asked.

"No, thank you," I was quick to say, answering for both of us.

"Suit yourselves," Wight said, grabbing a can of root beer out of the fridge. He pulled the tab and drank five long gulps without stopping for air, then sighed and wiped his lips with the back of his hand. "That's better."

If the state of his kitchen bothered Wight, he didn't show it. There was a doorway to the family room on my right and it didn't look nearly as messy. "Why don't we talk in there?" I asked, pointing to the family room.

Wight shrugged and nodded.

"But first," I said, "is it okay if I use your phone? I need to call my mom."

He eyed me skeptically and raised one of his thick eyebrows. "Thought all kids had cell phones these days."

"We do, but I forgot mine at home, and his stopped working while we were in the maze."

"It's still not working," Ryan said. "I think it's permanently fried or something."

Wight pointed to an old-fashioned phone mounted to the wall. "Go right ahead. You do know how to dial a rotary phone, don't you?"

"Of course he does," Ryan said.

"Right. Of course I do," I said. I didn't know what a rotary phone was, but how hard could it be? I picked up the handset and stared at the numbers positioned in circles on a clear dial.

Wight chuckled. "Put your finger inside the hole of the first number you want to dial and spin it all the way clockwise."

"I knew that," I said, sounding a little more defensive than I'd meant to. I spun the number two hole and the dial rotated back to its starting location. I dialed three, then six, then the rest of Mom's number.

The phone only rang once before Mom answered. "Hi, this is Kim—"

"Mom," I said quickly, "we need you to come get us—"

"—and I can't take your call right now. Please leave your name and number after the tone."

Of course. She must've turned her phone off for the movie. If I'd been able to text her she'd probably see it right away, but since that wasn't an option I left a voice message. It was better than nothing. I hung up the receiver with a *thud* that sounded too loud and final in the silence of the kitchen.

～っ૭Ꮾ᎒

Wight had positioned himself in a worn recliner chair across from Ryan and me, sitting side by side on a green plaid couch. He looked like he was trying to think of where to begin but couldn't quite make up his mind.

I looked around the room, trying my best to ignore the awkward silence. On the wall beside the brick fireplace was a large photograph of an aerial view of a maze. Beside that was a small curved blade and handle that had been hung on a pair of hooks. The blade looked like an antique farming tool.

"Is that your maze?" I asked, pointing at the photo.

"Yes," Wight said. "That was taken the first year I created it."

"Neat," I said, and I meant it. Even that first year the maze was impressively confusing, with countless paths zigzagging through the corn and leading to plenty of unforeseen dead ends. The paths of the top-left corner of the maze caught my eye. "Does that spell out Fall Fright?"

Wight smiled. "Sure does. I knew no one in the maze would see it, but I thought it would be fun to cut it that way."

The dot above the I in "Fright" was cut with no entrance to it, just like the clearing we'd accidentally discovered where Ryan had run into the scarecrow. I squinted at the picture and thought I could make out a scarecrow in the same spot that very first year.

Something else caught my attention. There was a piece of gray paper sticking out from behind the bottom corner of the picture.

"What's that?" I asked, pointing.

The chair squeaked as Wight swiveled to look. When he saw the paper, his eyes went wide and he stood quickly and yanked it free. It made a slight tearing sound as if it had been pinned to the wall behind the picture frame. It looked like an old newspaper article, but before I could get a good look at it, Wight stuffed it in his shirt pocket and said, "It's nothing. Never you mind."

I couldn't help but wonder why, if it was nothing, I had to "never you mind," but I knew it would be pointless to ask, so instead I asked another question.

"Why'd you first decide to create the maze?"

"The farm wasn't as profitable as it had once been," Wight said, turning his attention back to the picture. "I'd heard about other farms cutting corn mazes to draw in people, so I figured, why not? And it worked. I've made good money each year thanks to that maze. That first year, I used that small scythe"—he pointed at the curved blade on the wall—"and cut the entire pattern by hand. Took days. I started using large machinery a while back, but this year I had a few of my helpers cut the maze on their own. I just... I just couldn't be bothered anymore. But that's not what you came to hear. You asked how my cousin Clive died."

I nodded. "Did he die in the cornfield?"

"He did." Wight took a deep breath and let the air out slowly before continuing. "We were both ten years old and alone on the farm one afternoon. Bored as all get-out. Clive climbed up onto one of the tractors parked by the edge of the cornfield—it was the end of the season, so the corn had already been harvested—and said we should take it for a spin."

I thought of the tractor we'd seen parked beside the barn.

"My father had taught me how to operate it, of course, but he'd forbidden me to drive it without him. Clive didn't care about that. We were friends—shoot, he was my *best* friend—but he could be really stubborn until he got what he wanted. Not only that, but he could be pretty mean, too. Typical boy stuff, but it got under my skin. He started calling me a chicken and a baby—*bok-bok-bok* and *wah-wah-wah*, the way kids do—so finally I agreed to take the tractor out for five minutes, no more. Clive got all excited, so I started it up and off we went. But I was angry. I hated being called a chicken. I hated being called a baby!"

Ryan and I exchanged a concerned look. Wight had started shouting. His hands were balled into fists, and his cheeks and neck were red. Hyde was coming back.

Suddenly he got to his feet and began pacing back and forth through the room. "It was all his fault. If he hadn't been so insulting, I wouldn't have taken him out on the tractor." He stopped pacing in front of the picture of the maze and removed the hand scythe from the wall. He looked at it distractedly for a moment and then rested his right arm against the wall and pressed his forehead into his forearm. The blade, although old, gleamed in the light of the family room.

I had to struggle to hear his muffled voice when Wight spoke again.

"If Clive hadn't been so insulting, I wouldn't have killed him."

CHAPTER 15

"WHAT DID YOU SAY?" RYAN asked in a tone that made it clear he hadn't believed his own ears.

Wight didn't turn around to face us. "I said, if he hadn't been so insulting, he wouldn't have died."

Ryan opened his mouth to correct Wight, to inform him that he'd said something quite different, but I quickly grabbed his shoulder and raised a finger to my lips to make him keep quiet.

The silence stretched out between us, and I

had to resist the urge to break it by saying something, but I figured that if Ryan and I waited long enough Wight would eventually tell us more.

"We were going no more than ten miles per hour, so it shouldn't have been dangerous," Wight said, still leaning against the wall. "But then..."

He fell silent again, and since I still couldn't see his face I couldn't tell if he was sad, mad or something else. But when he started talking again I could hear the emotion in his voice. He was scared.

"A few feet dead ahead of the tractor, I saw a skull. A human skull. I gave the steering wheel a hard yank to my left to avoid it. Clive, who was seated on my right, flew off the seat and tumbled out of sight. I brought the tractor to a sudden stop, jumped off it, and found my cousin lying in the field. I rolled him over and saw that he had injured his head. Beside his body was a rock coated in his blood—he must've landed headfirst on it. He might've survived if not for that. And like a punch to the gut I realized that what I'd swerved to avoid was the rock Clive had smashed his head on. The shape of the rock looked like it had a pair of eyes, and I'd foolishly mistaken it for something it clearly wasn't."

Could the rock that killed Clive have been the same one we'd left beside the scarecrow in the maze?

Wight shook his head and then, in a softer voice that made it seem like he wasn't speaking to us, he said, "That's the truth of what happened, regardless of how many people had their doubts."

I wasn't surprised to hear Wight say people had their doubts about his version of how Clive died. I was beginning to have some doubts myself. I needed answers and wondered where I might find them.

The bedroom with the picture of Clive, I suddenly thought.

"I have to go to the bathroom," I announced. Ryan looked at me with a hint of fear. He probably didn't want to be left alone with Wight, and I couldn't say that I blamed him for that. I shrugged and said, "Too much Slushee." And then I held up my index finger and silently mouthed the words, "I'll be one minute."

Wight turned around and waved his hand—the one that held the scythe—as if casually dismissing me from class.

I stood up and walked to the door.

Wight cleared his throat to stop me. "You know where it is?" he asked.

I nodded, smiled agreeably, and said, "Yeah, sure. I saw it when we came in. Down the hallway, near the front door."

"Straight there and back," he said in a warning tone.

"Of course," I said lightly, trying to keep a calm exterior.

I walked quickly along the hallway without pausing to peek into the bedroom, turning to look back at the family room once I'd reached the front. I couldn't see Wight, and he couldn't see me, but I wasn't taking any chances. I turned on the bathroom light and closed the door, then crept as silently as possible back to the bedroom.

I approached the desk and stared at Clive's picture for a moment. It was surrounded by trinkets and toys, knickknacks and random objects, like a shrine.

There was a small bulletin board on the wall behind the desk. Pinned to it was a short article cut out of a newspaper, a small rectangle curled and yellowed by time. It was Clive's obituary.

WIGHT-CLIVE, beloved son of Victor and Selma, died in a farming accident. Memorial service, family only. Sunday noon at home, Kelowna. No flowers.

Was the article that had been hidden behind the picture of the corn maze also something to do with Clive's death? I leaned against the table as I read the short and rather sad obituary. *Baddest of them all.* That's what Clive had said when he'd seen...not the bad man, but Wight approaching. Before he'd turned and fled in fear. A wave of nausea passed through me, the feeling once again that I was no longer alone.

"What are you doing in here?" Wight said in a low, slow growl from the open doorway behind me.

CHAPTER 16

WIGHT TOOK A THREATENING STEP toward me as I turned to face him. My eyes were immediately drawn to the scythe. He held it in his left hand. I thought he might not even be aware he still held it. But that could change at any moment.

"You didn't have to go to the bathroom at all, did you?" he asked. "You came in here on purpose, didn't you?"

I shook my head but didn't answer. What could I say? I made a wrong turn? He'd see right through that. Instead, I weighed my options and looked for a way out. The room had one window, but it was boarded up with a piece of plywood nailed to the frame. I thought I could race to it before Wight could catch me, but would I be able to pull the board down? Or would I feel his blade dig into my back before I got out?

The risk was too great. I had to try to talk my way out.

"Okay, listen—"

"No, you listen!" Wight shouted. He pointed the blade at me. He took another step.

Run, I thought. *Knock him down.* I tried to command my body to move, but I was frozen to the spot.

"Straight there, straight back," Wight said, an angry blotch of red seeping up his neck. "You shouldn't have come in here. You've seen too much." He still hadn't lowered the scythe.

Since I wasn't capable of moving my feet, I raised my hands in the air. "I'm sorry. I took a wrong turn, but I don't know what you're talking about. I haven't seen anything."

"Not only are you a sneak, but you're a liar, too." His eyes flicked to the table, the shrine he'd created to his murdered cousin, and I knew then that he wasn't going to let me go.

Luckily, Ryan stepped into the room and swung a fire poker as hard as he could. It struck Wight on the back of the head. His eyes rolled upward, and he crumpled to the floor in a heap, facedown.

Ryan looked down at Wight and smiled. "That felt good," he said.

"Thanks," I said. "He has this weird shrine to his cousin in here. I don't think Clive's death was an accident."

"Oh, so now you agree with me that he's a killer, eh?"

I shrugged. "Yeah. Um...sorry for insisting we come in here."

"Well, he hasn't killed us yet, so I'll let you off the hook just this once."

Creak!

It was the sound of the floorboards groaning. Ryan hadn't moved, and neither had I. We both shut up, held our breaths, and stared at Wight for a tense moment.

"Was that him?" I whispered. Ryan shrugged.

I doubted getting whacked on the back of the head with a poker would have improved Wight's mood. We needed to get out of the house before he woke up.

Creak!

There it was again, but this time I'd been looking at Wight, and he hadn't moved a muscle.

There was someone else in the house.

Ryan stepped out of the room, looked down the hall, and flinched. He looked like he'd seen a ghost. He turned to face me, and the expression on his face was one of pure terror—I'd never seen anything like it in my life.

"Hide," he whispered urgently. And then he

sprinted down the hall to his left. Away from whatever he'd seen. Whatever had scared him so badly.

I dove under the bed. From there I could see a man walk past the bedroom. The bad man. Who was he? And what did he want with us?

His large feet plodded by, creaking the floorboards with every step, and then he was gone. He hadn't noticed Wight. He also hadn't run, so I hoped Ryan could quickly find a place to hide. I hoped he'd be okay. Who knew what would happen to my cousin if the bad man caught up to him? I needed to help Ryan, and to do that I had to get out of Wight's house immediately.

I slid out from under the bed and tried pulling down the piece of plywood nailed to the window frame. No luck. The board didn't budge. It would take a crowbar to get it off.

That left me one option. I had to go over Wight to get through the doorway.

But what if he was faking? What if he was

waiting for me to move closer so that he could hack at my legs with his scythe?

It didn't matter. There was no other way out— and I needed to get out.

I balled my hands into fists, clenched my teeth, and slowly approached Wight.

CHAPTER 17

DAD USED TO SING "WE'RE Going on a Bear Hunt" every time we'd set out for a walk through the woods.

Even that final time we'd gone on a hike.

He'd told me that most bears are more afraid of humans than we are of them, but I'd always felt that singing that song was tempting fate. I didn't want to come face-to-face with a bear on its home turf, regardless of how scared it might be of us.

As I eyed Wight's unmoving body between me

and the hallway, an altered version of the song played in my head.

Going on a ghost hunt.

Gonna catch a big one.

I'm not scared.

What a beautiful day.

But it wasn't a beautiful day, I wasn't what you would call "not scared," and I had no intention of hunting the bad man (although he was a big one, that much was true), so I had to wonder why my mind had chosen that moment to pull the song up from the depths of my memory and toy around with its lyrics.

Oh no! A killer blocking my path!

Can't go through him.

Can't go around him.

Can't go under him.

Have to go over him!

And there it was, the big reveal and the connection between something my dad used to sing and this mess I was in.

But the song—and my subconscious, I guess—weren't wrong. There was no other way out. I had to go over him.

You can do this, I told myself. *Just jump over him and get out. Now!*

He moved. His left leg spasmed.

I froze, my muscles tense and my jaw clenched.

Was he waking up?

I steadied my nerves and prepared to jump, but then I spotted something.

The newspaper article from behind the maze picture that Wight didn't want me to see. It was sticking out from under his leg. It must have slipped out of his pocket when he fell to the ground.

Instead of running away, I crouched down and grabbed the corner of the clipping, then pulled it as I stood up.

But the newspaper was old and brittle. The corner ripped, leaving the article beneath Mr. Wight's leg and a tiny piece pinched between my finger and thumb.

The old man groaned—a horrible sound, more animal than human—and shifted his body. No doubt about it; he was waking up.

And things had gone from bad to worse. When he'd moved, he'd rolled over, completely covering the article. I could no longer see it at all.

That's it, I thought. *Forget it. Run.*

"No," I said quietly through gritted teeth, shaking my head.

If Ryan had been there I'm sure he would have looked at me like I had totally lost it. Based on what I was thinking of doing, I probably had.

No time to lose. I slid both my hands under Wight's leg and rolled him over with a grunt. It freed the newspaper article.

It also woke Wight.

I grabbed the article. He grabbed my arm.

He tightened his grip on my sleeve and tried to pull me closer but I unzipped my jacket and slipped out of it, simultaneously freeing myself from his grasp and sending him backward. He fell on the ground holding my discarded jacket and cursed loudly.

I bolted through the doorway and tore off down the hall, heading in the same direction Ryan had run. The front door was slightly ajar, so I figured he'd probably left the house and was hiding somewhere outside.

"Wait!" Wight shouted from behind me as I ran to the door. "Get back here so I can explain something!"

Not a chance. I knew it was a trap, and besides, I had the article. Without slowing down I pushed open the door and flew down the front porch steps and nearly ran straight into a group of five or six older kids who were walking by.

"Watch it, idiot!" one of the bigger boys said.

I didn't answer or slow down, but darted behind the house for cover. I didn't know which way Ryan went once he left the house so I needed time to think.

Would he have gone into the petting zoo? The

pumpkin patch? Surely he wouldn't have gone back into the maze. Would he?

Five or six minutes passed as I tried to think things through. Suddenly I heard a loud mechanical screech that made me jump. I peered around the corner of the house and saw the guy who'd pretended to have been killed in the ticket booth walk into the open field that served as the hub to all of Fall Fright's attractions. Axe Head held a megaphone to his mouth and turned in a slow circle as he spoke.

"Fall Fright is now closed," he said, his voice booming through the horn. "I repeat, Fall Fright is now closed. Everyone must leave immediately."

The few small clusters of people I could see from where I stood stopped, looked from Axe Head to each other and held quiet, confused conversations, but none of them made to leave. My best guess was that it was probably eight thirty or nine; Fall Fright stayed open until midnight, so people who had paid to be there were obviously reluctant to leave.

Axe Head sighed into the megaphone and then said, "I've been told you'll receive a full refund at the ticket booth if you go now."

That did the trick. After a very short pause for the new info to sink in, everyone happily made their way quickly toward the exit. Apparently, no one had been having such a good time that they'd rather stay than get their money back to leave.

It seemed pretty obvious to me that Wight had closed the farm. Could I use the mass exodus as a distraction to sneak out? Maybe, but there wasn't a chance I was leaving without Ryan. And there was the real possibility that Wight was hiding somewhere near the exit, waiting for me.

A blur of shadow moved through the trees to my right. My breath caught in my throat. Whatever it was hadn't made a sound.

"Who's there?" I asked in a hushed voice,

hopeful it was my cousin but fearful it was the bad man. "Ryan?"

A boy stepped into view, but it wasn't my cousin. It was Clive, walking over dry leaves and twigs in perfect silence.

"Oh, it's you," I said, both a little disappointed and a little relieved. "Have you seen my cousin? I don't know where he went. Or have you seen *your* cousin? He's trying to kill me, and I know he..."

I was going to say, "and I know he killed you," but I trailed off. A horrible look of fear twisted Clive's face as he pointed over my shoulder.

I turned and saw what—or rather who—Clive had seen.

Standing behind me, looking like he was three seconds away from a complete meltdown, was Wight.

"There you are," he said.

CHAPTER 18

"STAY BACK!" I SHOUTED, BUT the words sounded hollow. It was an empty threat and Wight knew it. He had the scythe. I had nothing. My only option was to run.

"Wait," Wight said, not angered, not yelling. "Wait," he repeated softly, almost pleadingly.

His tone and his expression made me hesitate. "I'm not going to hurt you," he said.

My eyes darted to his scythe, and his followed mine. He dropped the blade beside his feet, then raised his empty hands.

I kept my body tensed and ready to run at a moment's notice. Just in case. After all, the ghost of his murder victim was standing right behind me and I didn't want to end up like Clive.

I turned and looked at Clive, expecting to see a look of blind terror on his face. But instead he was smiling, and a tear rolled down his cheek.

"What do you want?" I asked Wight, turning back around to face him.

"The only thing I want," he said, "is to see my cousin again. To tell him..." He craned his head to look around me. To look at Clive. "I'm sorry."

Sorry for murdering him sixty years ago? I thought bitterly. *It's a little late for that.*

"I'm sorry, too," Clive said.

"Huh?" I said, but no one was listening to me.

Wight and Clive walked toward each other and met a few feet from where I stood. Wight crouched down and opened his arms for a hug but Clive held up a hand.

"If I touch you it'll hurt real bad," he said. "It could even kill you."

Wight nodded. "It's so good to see you again, Clive."

"You too, Edgar."

"I've missed you," Wight said. "All this time I've... I've felt horrible for what happened."

"It wasn't your fault. We shouldn't have driven the tractor. That was *my* fault. And the fact that you turned and I fell out... Well, that was nobody's fault."

"I thought..." I said, figuring things out and realizing that Wight had told the truth about how Clive died.

"I know what you thought," Wight said. He was eyeing me with a hint of annoyance but also without any hate. "And I can understand why you thought it. I've been beating myself up for what happened for more than sixty years, and sometimes I have a hard time controlling my emotions. I recognize that sometimes I come across as a little aggressive. Maybe even a little scary."

I didn't disagree with his self-assessment. "When that guy told everyone to go home I thought it meant I was in trouble—even more trouble than I already was."

"I sent everyone home so I could look for Clive," Wight said. "I didn't want anyone—other than you—to find him first. What would people think if they bumped into a *real* ghost at Fall Fright? But I'm sure I'll get some complaints about closing early."

Angry letters, I thought, remembering the parents who had stormed out as Ryan and I had entered Fall Fright.

"But I don't care," Wight added. He looked at Clive. "I only care that you're back. But speaking of which, how *did* you get back?"

Clive shook his head. "I have no idea. A portal opened up in the cornfield a little while ago, and I was able to pass through."

"A portal?" I asked.

With a nod, Clive said, "One of the ways that can happen is if part of a deceased person's remains are returned to the location where they died." He looked at me, and I looked at Wight.

Wight, in turn, looked at the boarded-up window that led to the room with the shrine. "Next to the picture of Clive in my bedroom, along with the few things of his I have, I kept the rock that he hit when he fell out of the trac- tor." Wight raised his hands defensively. "I know how that sounds, and looks, but it's served as a reminder of what happened that day and the part I played in Clive's death. Well, yesterday I threw the rock through the window in a fit of rage. When I came to my senses and ran outside to retrieve it, I couldn't find it."

"You have to let it go, Edgar," Clive said. "You have to stop beating yourself up for what happened to me. Your guilt is why I can't move on, why I've been stuck in the Netherrealm all these years."

Wight nodded and took off his hat, then twisted it in his hands as he thought. "The rock has some of your dried blood on it, but I didn't take it anywhere near the cornfield. So how did the portal open today?"

There was a lot to unpack in what they'd both just said, but I figured I should start with the rock. I raised my hand slowly in the air, which immediately grabbed the cousins' attention. "Um. I found the rock."

"Where?" Wight asked.

I pointed at the weeds where I'd found it.

"Did you take it into the cornfield?" Clive asked. Technically speaking Ryan did, but I decided to not throw him under the bus and nodded. "I guess I accidentally opened the portal to the... What did you call it?"

"The Netherrealm," Clive said.

"Wait a minute," Wight said. He set his hat back on his head. "You also came back thirteen years ago, but the rock was in my house the entire time."

Thirteen years ago, I thought. *That was the first year the maze opened. Clive returned that year, too?*

Clive looked at Wight and cocked his head to the side. "Were you holding the rock before you entered the maze that night?"

Wight thought for a moment before his eyes widened. "Cutting the maze brought back some painful memories," he admitted. "Yeah, I'd been holding the rock and thinking back, and then I walked out to the maze. I spent some time at the scene of your accident, the dot of the I in 'Fall Fright,' looking up at the moon. I must've had some of your blood on my hands, and I guess I brushed it off."

"That must be how the portal first opened," Clive said.

There was something bugging me, something I couldn't wait any longer to ask Clive. "When I saw you earlier this evening, you said your cousin was the 'baddest of them all.' What did you mean by that?"

Wight's head tilted back in surprise and Clive frowned. "No, I didn't," he said.

"Yes, you did," I said gently. "We heard someone coming, I asked if it was the bad man—"

"The bad man?" Wight asked, but I continued. "You nodded and said it was the baddest of them all, disappeared, and then your cousin broke through the corn."

"I thought it was Kane," Clive said. "Everyone in the Netherrealm calls him the bad man. The things I've seen him do... There's no one worse; that's why I said he's the baddest of them all."

"Kane," Wight said. His eyes looked both far away and intensely concerned. "I know that name."

"He's obsessed with returning here and has been searching for a way through ever since I first saw him thirteen years ago. The portal you opened," Clive told Wight, "only remained open for a short time. I traveled through and tried to find you—I'm pretty sure I scared a lot of people in the maze—but as soon as I reached your house and saw you sitting on your front porch, I felt the portal closing and had to return. It closed just as I slipped back through, and that's when I first saw Kane."

Wight gave this a little thought, then pointed at my tense left hand and said, "Look at that, and show my cousin, too."

I unclenched my fist and looked at the balled-up newspaper article with a little bit of astonishment. I'd forgotten I still had it. I gently spread the paper flat and was shocked to find an old black-and-white photograph of the bad man staring back at me. I showed Clive, who nodded.

"That's him," he said.

"Go ahead and read it," Wight said.

ALLEGED
ATTEMPTED MURDER

At the Kelowna Court Monday Jonathan Kane, 38, of Kelowna, was charged with having attempted to murder John and Harriet Tully.

On September 24, the Tullys were driving north of the city when their automobile broke down. The couple cut through Kane's cornfield as they approached the farm, seeking aid. They were startled when Kane exited his house brandishing a shotgun and yelled at them.

Harriet claims Kane said, "This here's private property and I'll defend it to my dying day. And when that day comes I'll find a way back!" He then fired the shotgun at the startled couple as they ran back to their automobile.

Kane's lawyer, Henry Northmore, argued that his client had no intent of killing either Tully and that his was a warning shot aimed well above their

heads. The accused will reappear in
court on Friday.

"Kane was found guilty," Wight said once I
looked up from the article, "and spent two years
in jail. He lost the farm, and my parents bought
it from the bank before I was born. Kane hated
my family after that, and my father warned me
to stay away from him at all costs. I've lived most
of my life in fear of a man I've never met. I even
feared him after I'd heard he'd died. In truth, I
feared him a little more. Sometimes when I was
alone in the cornfield, late at night, I thought
I heard a deep, gruff voice calling my name.
Part of me always thought it was Kane." Wight
laughed and looked around anxiously. "My father
pinned the article to the wall to remind himself
to be careful out there, and he left it up even after
Kane died. I never got around to asking him why.
It always made me uncomfortable, so I hung the
picture of the maze over top. For some reason I

could never bring myself to take it down." His nervous gaze settled on the entrance to the corn maze.

"Well, now Kane is back," Clive said, "and the years spent in the Netherrealm haven't made him any nicer."

"What exactly is the Netherrealm?" I asked.

"It's the place between this world and the next," Clive said. "Some souls—innocent ones— get trapped there. Others—the not-so-innocent ones—choose to stay there so they can try to get back here."

I knew exactly which camp Kane fell into. "Ever since I saw you come out of the maze all those years ago, I've been trying to bring you back," Wight told Clive as he picked the scythe back up. "I thought maybe that cutting the maze had somehow done it, so I cut the exact same pattern year after year. This year I was starting to lose hope."

Old Man Wight, I thought. *Obsessed with his*

corn maze. Well, now I knew why. But it didn't matter. Ryan was still somewhere out there, and so was Kane.

"Kane followed Ryan out of the house," I said. "I don't know where either of them went. I think Ryan might be in danger."

"I saw your cousin run into the maze not too long ago," Clive said. "But I'm afraid stopping Kane isn't as easy as you'd think. If we remove the rock it'll close the portal, yes, but it'll close it with Kane on this side."

"What are you saying?" I asked, fearing the answer.

Clive looked paler than usual. "Somehow— don't ask me how—we need to force Kane back through the portal before closing it."

CHAPTER 19

NOT THE CORN MAZE, ANYWHERE but the corn maze, I thought to myself as we entered the corn maze.

But there was no other option. Ryan was in there. So was the portal to the Netherrealm. And so was Kane.

Which was the reason I didn't want to go back into the corn maze.

Wight, Clive, and I passed under the scythe at the entrance and walked as quickly as possible as we traveled deeper into the maze, searching for that bizarre area where Wight had cut the paths to spell out "Fall Fright." The place where Clive had died, and Ryan and I had allowed Kane to return to our world.

We moved in silence with Wight in the lead, but even he didn't seem to know how to get to the portal. We ran into a dead end, stopped, and backtracked a little. Hit another dead end, turned around, and ran blindly forward. Every shadow looked like Kane, every creak of the stalks sounded like his feet creeping up behind us, stalking us, preparing to pounce...

Wight looked both confused and a little flustered. "I thought I knew exactly where to go—I mean, it's my maze—but this cornfield has a habit of tricking you."

I knew what he meant.

Around and around we turned, left, right, left, right, quickly tiring and growing disoriented. Every passage, each turn—they all began to look the same. I couldn't remember where we'd been and had no idea which way to go. We turned another corner, and the temperature plummeted.

"Wait," I said. I stopped running.

Clive looked back at me. "What is it? Kane?"

"No," I said, the word punctuated by a cloud of breath in front of my face. "See that? It's cold. Too cold."

Wight exhaled heavily and a long, cloudy stream of frosty air came out of his mouth. No foggy breath came from Clive, I noticed.

"Kane must be nearby. Let's keep going." I sprinted around a corner and looked back, then came to a sudden stop.

Neither Wight nor Clive had followed me. It was as if they had disappeared. I was alone.

The cornstalks rustled together and the stars blinked overhead.

"Clive?" I called out. "Mr. Wight?"

"I have your cousin," a deep voice said.

I spun around, still alone. The voice must

have come from the shadows between the stalks, but where? "Who said that?"

"You know who."

Kane. His voice seemed to circle me as he spoke. "Let Ryan go and we'll leave," I said.

"But why would I *let* you leave?" Kane said. "We're just getting started."

Kane suddenly emerged from a slim space between two cornstalks. His irises and pupils were as black as tar except for a small white point of light that swirled deep within each.

I turned to run, but he grabbed my wrist. My skin immediately felt like it was on fire, just like before. I yelled in pain and fell to my knees, my head spinning and my body freezing.

Not again, I thought desperately. I tried to yank my arm free but it was useless. I couldn't move.

Kane leaned in close, his teeth only an inch or two from my ear. "This time, I'm not going to let you go, and there's nothing you can do to stop me."

The world grew darker with every labored heartbeat. I was losing consciousness quickly.

Through the fog in my head I heard footsteps approach. I saw a shadowy figure swing something at Kane.

Kane let go of my wrist and bellowed in rage.

My vision returned to normal.

It was Wight. He'd swung the scythe at Kane. The blade had grazed Kane's bicep. His skin sizzled and gray smoke drifted through the tear in his shirt. He cupped his hand over the wound and flew through a wall of corn.

Wight's smile fell from his face as soon as he looked at my chest.

I looked down and felt all the blood drain from my face as I saw what had scared him so badly.

From my left side to my right, just above my belly, there was a long, deep gash through the front of my shirt.

The scythe hadn't only cut Kane's arm. It had also cut me. I raised my sweater and T-shirt and was relieved to find that the scythe had sliced my clothes but not my body. I didn't have so much as a scratch on my skin.

But my relief was short-lived. Kane was back, turning a corner at the end of the passage and running straight for us.

CHAPTER 20

I BLINKED AND REALIZED THAT it wasn't Kane approaching. It was Ryan.

Overcome with relief, I opened my mouth to tell Ryan I was so thankful to see him, but he noticed Clive and Wight, then the cut across my chest, then the scythe in Wight's hand.

"What have you done?" he demanded of Wight. "Get away from him!"

"It's okay. I'm not hurt. He's not a bad guy," I told Ryan from where I lay on the ground. "He didn't kill Clive, and this happened," I pointed at the cut in my shirt, "when he saved me from Kane. It was an accident."

"I thought I had..." Wight said quietly.

I slowly got to my feet. The fog began to clear from my head and I still felt impossibly cold, as if Kane's touch had coated my bones in frost, but at least he was gone. For now.

"You saved me," I told Wight.

He nodded but still apologized for good measure.

"Kane said he had caught you," I told Ryan.

He shook his head. "Nah. I'm seriously winded, and I've got the worst cramp of my life, but I managed to evade him. Still, I don't ever want to run or jog or even walk fast ever again. So what now?"

I filled Ryan in on how we (well, technically speaking, *he*) had accidentally opened a portal to the Netherrealm when the rock he'd placed on the scarecrow had fallen, and how that had allowed Kane to return to this world, and how Kane hated people being on what he still considered to be his property, and how we now needed to knock him back through the portal before closing it.

Ryan bent over, informed us he thought he was going to puke, counted to ten, and then stood up, took three deep breaths, and apologized for unknowingly opening the portal. All things considered, I thought he took it pretty well.

"Well, what are we waiting for?" he asked. "Let's go to the scarecrow."

"Small problem," I said. "We're having trouble finding it."

"Then it's a good thing I found you when I did, because I was just there." Ryan hitched his thumb over his shoulder, down the path he'd just come from. "Back a little way I found some bent cornstalks, and sure enough it led to that clearing. I camped out there for a bit while I caught my breath before I heard you guys."

I patted Ryan on the back of the shoulder. "Lead the way."

We took two steps, but Kane's voice stopped us all cold.

"If you think that I'm going to sit back and let you plot against me," Kane growled, unseen from within the corn, "think again."

Goose bumps pricked my skin. Like before, his voice had come from four directions at once. I might've thought he was speaking directly into my head if not for the fact that Ryan, Wight, and Clive all heard Kane's voice, too.

"Stop being such a chicken and show yourself," Wight said. Part of me respected him a little more, and part of me wished he hadn't said that.

"All in good time. But first, I have to make up my mind about something very important. I have to decide how best to get rid of everyone trespassing on my property, starting with the four of you."

"Not a chance," Wight said.

"And who's going to stop me?" Kane asked. "An old man and three kids?" He laughed hollowly.

Ryan, Wight, and I huddled close together in the center of the path, our backs touching. Clive was careful not to touch us. I could feel Ryan and Wight shaking behind me. I was shaking, too.

"We haven't done anything to you," I said. "Neither have any of the other people visiting the farm tonight. And it's not even your farm anymore. Mr. Wight owns it now, so you have no right to say who can be here and who can't."

"You might have a point," Kane said, and for a brief moment I was genuinely shocked. But then he added, "But I don't care."

And I knew at that moment that any shred of reason that Kane had had in life—if he'd had any at all—had completely evaporated during the time he'd spent in the Netherrealm. There was no sense trying to talk to him any further.

Snap!

"I've got an idea," Kane said. And then he laughed. And then...nothing.

Silence.

"Kane?" I said.

No response.

"Is he gone?" Ryan asked.

"Yes, but he'll be back," Clive said.

"What now?" Ryan asked.

Our best plan was still our first plan, even if it was far from fully formed. But how could I knock Kane into the portal if I couldn't even touch him?

And then I had an idea. "Hey guys," I said, but before I could tell the others what I was thinking I heard Kane returning. He was whistling, as if he didn't have a care in the world. As if he wasn't planning on killing everyone at Fall Fright.

"I'm back," he said, still not revealing himself. "Did you miss me?"

No one answered.

"Fall Fright," Kane said with a tone of disgust. "Since you're all going to die here in this corn maze, I figured that should play a significant part in your end."

Kane floated out of the cornstalks to our right. He held something in his hands that bent the corn and made me forget all about my idea. It wouldn't work. Nothing would. We were dead meat, just like Kane wanted.

In his hands he held a scythe, plucked from the scarecrow at the entrance to the maze, so large that it made Wight's scythe look like a child's toy.

CHAPTER 21

KANE TOOK A STEP TOWARD us and raised the scythe in the air, preparing to swing it straight at my chest.

My idea will still work, I told myself. I shouldn't have lost hope. I couldn't give up.

"You try to cut me down with that," I said, reaching out and ripping the small scythe free from Wight's hand, "and I'll throw this at you. Remember what happened when he cut your arm? Hurt, didn't it? And this time I'll make sure it goes straight through your chest, or better yet, your head."

That gave Kane pause. His smile faded, and he lowered his scythe slightly. That was good.

"You'll miss," he said.

"I won't," I guaranteed. "I could hit you with my eyes closed." I hoped my tone was confident, but my hand was shaking so badly I worried he'd see it and call my bluff.

Kane lowered his scythe a little farther, and I could see in his black eyes that he was afraid.

"So what now?" he said, eyeing me warily. "I'll never let you all leave alive."

"What about a deal?" I said.

"A deal?" Wight asked me. He seemed upset at the thought of striking a deal with Kane.

"What sort of deal?" Kane said.

"Let us go to the Netherrealm."

"Why do you want to go there?" Kane said.

"My dad died last year, and I want to see him one last time. After that, well, you can do whatever you want with us." I didn't dare look at the others, too afraid they might protest and give away the lie, but Kane seemed to buy it.

"Fine," Kane said. "But just so you know, you'll be responsible for anything that happens to anyone still here on my farm." He gave Wight a withering look and tightened his grip on the scythe's handle.

"If I get to see my father one last time," I said, hating that I was using my dad like that, "it'll be worth it."

"Go now before I change my mind," Kane said.

"There's no time to explain," I whispered to Clive and Wight, and then turned to Ryan. "Quick, take us to the scarecrow."

Ryan gave me a doubtful look but led us down the path, around the corner and into the corn where we'd broken a path earlier in the night. Kane waited and watched until we could no longer see him.

"You know he'll never let us go, right?" Wight said.

"He's going to follow us," Clive added.

"I'm planning on it," I said. "I want him to follow us, and when he's close enough to the portal I'll hit him with this." I indicated the hand scythe.

"You're going to need luck on your side," Ryan said.

"Tell me about it," I said.

We broke into the hidden clearing with the scarecrow. Across the way, just behind the first row of cornstalks that made up the opposite wall, I spotted a patch in the air that was darker than dark. I'd seen it briefly when we'd first been there, just after I had thought I'd heard and seen my dad. I didn't think much of it back then, but now I knew it was the entrance to the Netherrealm. And I paused. I paused and considered—seriously considered—that my dad might be somewhere in that darkness. He might not have passed on, like Clive and Kane. I might actually have the ability to see him, to speak with him, to spend a little more time with him. Even one second would be... Well, it would be beyond words.

I shook my head. None of that was possible. Kane needed to be sent back to the Netherrealm.

I wondered if we'd need to pretend to be going through with the act of trying to contact my dad so that our cover wouldn't be blown, but I didn't need to wonder any further.

Kane stepped out from the corn and stood between us and the portal.

"On second thought, I'm afraid I can't honor my end of the deal," he said. "Not only are you two a couple of trespassers"—he pointed at Ryan and me—"but he has no right to this property. *My* property. And for that—"

I didn't let him finish, and I didn't give him any warning. I threw the scythe at him. It sailed through the air, end over end, making a *whoosh-whoosh-whoosh* sound with each revolution.

He dropped his own scythe and ducked.

My scythe missed. Only by a hair, but it missed and flew into the Netherrealm.

Gone.

"Oh no," I said. I'd intended to knock him backward into the Netherrealm, hoping that would buy us enough time to grab the rock and take it as far away from this bit of land as possible. But now I was left standing there, hands empty and out of ideas.

Kane laughed.

"I told you you'd miss," he said.

He flew toward me. He was moving so fast that I didn't have time to run away.

But Clive picked up Kane's scythe from the ground and leapt forward. He swung it just as Kane's fingers were barely an inch from my throat. The scythe hit him in his midsection and its effect was instantaneous.

Kane stopped and arched backward. He howled in pain—an unearthly sound that sent shock waves through the night. His chest dissolved into a swirl of bright mist. Before long his entire body evaporated, from his head to his toes, and what was left of him—the mist—floated up into the sky. I lost sight of it among the stars overhead.

"Is he...dead?" I asked.

Clive nodded. "I think so."

"How did that kill him?" Ryan asked.

"Ghosts are repelled by iron," Clive said. "I can hold the wooden handle, like Kane, but the blade... Well, you saw what happened." He threw the scythe hard to the dirt as if he was suddenly repulsed by it.

"Thank you both so very much," Clive said, smiling at me and Ryan.

"So what now?" Ryan said, turning to face me.

I picked up the rock. "We have to get this far away to close the portal again." But then I realized there'd always be a risk the portal could be opened again, and who knows what other spirits were lurking in the Netherrealm, waiting for their chance to return to our world. An idea suddenly struck me. "And I know just the place to put it to make sure the portal never opens again."

"Where?" Ryan asked.

"In there." I pointed at the portal, at the Netherrealm.

No one said anything for a moment, but then Clive nodded and said, "That's a good idea. A really good idea."

"But that means you won't be able to travel back and forth," Wight said. "That means you'll be stuck here forever."

"No," Clive said, shaking his head. "I feel like I'm ready to move on, into the Netherrealm and then on to whatever lies beyond it. Your guilt isn't holding me here anymore."

Wight was silent for a moment before he sucked in a deep breath of air, nodded once, and said, "Yes. I'm ready, too. No more holding on to the past. No more obsessing over this maze." He exhaled and immediately looked happier, more relaxed, and five or ten years younger.

"You don't have to obsess over it," I said, "but you can definitely keep creating it, right?" I knew it was a bit of a selfish request, but now that I'd gotten over my fear of returning without my dad I couldn't imagine *not* returning next year, and for years to come.

"Oh, I'll definitely keep on running Fall Fright," Wight said without hesitation. "It makes far too much money for me to stop, and think what the rumor that the corn maze is haunted by real ghosts will do for business."

"They're the only two people who know what really happened here tonight," Clive said, pointing at Ryan and me.

Wight winked at us. "And I have no doubt the rumor will spread, won't it, boys?"

"You got it," I said.

Clive thanked us again for what we did to put a stop to Kane, then stepped into the black patch within the corn. He turned to face us, waved goodbye, and nodded as he faded from view. I took that to mean he was ready.

So did Ryan. He picked up the rock.

"Ready?" I asked Ryan and Wight, but mostly Wight.

They both nodded.

And then, without any further fanfare, Ryan threw the rock into the darkness of the Netherrealm. The portal sealed shut immediately.

"So..." Ryan said. "Is that it?"

"I think so," I said.

Wight tried to hide wiping a tear out of the corner of his eye. "I do hope Clive is able to move on now, like he wanted," he said quietly.

"Do you mind," I asked him, "if we use your phone again?"

"Of course," Wight said. He cleared his throat and spoke up a bit. "But this time, don't go off snooping around my house when you say you're going to the bathroom, all right?"

"All right," I said with a laugh.

CHAPTER 22

IT WAS ONE OF THOSE perfect autumn days. The air was cool and crisp but the sun was bright and warm. My lungs burned pleasantly with every breath and my skin tingled as if I was sitting in the glow of a roaring fire.

Mom, Grace, and I came to a steep cliff and looked down at the creek below. It twisted through the forest like a long, thin snake, carrying ice-cold water from the peaks of the Rocky Mountains. For a moment we all just stared at the sparkling water and enjoyed the peaceful bubbling of the creek, taking our time and absorbing the tranquility of the moment. We'd hiked for a little more than an hour, and now that we were so close to our destination, a few extra minutes wouldn't hurt. I set my backpack down gently at my feet, and Mom and Grace both followed suit. The contents of Grace's backpack rattled loudly.

"What do you have in there?" I asked her.

Grace met my eyes briefly and then looked back down at the creek. "Oh, you know, just some toys Dad and I used to play with."

"That's cool." I'd also put a few things in my backpack that reminded me of him.

I'd missed my dad even more than I had allowed myself to realize. During the week after Fall Fright, my dad was just about all I could think about. I kept picturing the rock with Clive's blood and the rift in the air between the cornstalks that led to the Netherrealm, and this persistent idea came to me. It wriggled into my brain like a worm, a worm that refused to leave. I couldn't shake it. Could we use Dad's ashes to open a portal where he'd died? Could we see him again?

After a few long, obsessive days, I came to a firm resolution: I could never, ever try to bring Dad back. He might not even be in the Netherrealm. And what if opening a portal allowed another spirit like Kane to return? The thought gave me goose bumps. If the events I'd lived through at Fall Fright had taught me one thing, it was that there are things in this world we can't understand, and forces we shouldn't mess with. I didn't have to like that Dad died, but I had to accept it. And I had to move on.

It was what he would have wanted. So when Mom suggested we all go for a hike in Rose Valley Park, I agreed. I was ready.

I took one last look at the creek below and picked up my backpack. So did Mom and Grace, the toys rattling loudly again.

"You two ready to move on?" Mom asked. Grace and I both nodded.

We made our way carefully down the sloped path. We reached the bottom and walked beside the creek for a while until we came to the clearing.

Everything looked just as I remembered it from that awful day nearly a year ago. Red maple trees formed a wide horseshoe beside the creek. The green grass surrounded a large, flat rock, perfect for sitting on and taking a break during a hike. It had taken Mom, Grace, and me a moment to notice there was something wrong with Dad. He leaned against the rock and clutched his chest, but he didn't make a sound. The next thing I knew, Dad was lying on the ground and Mom was kneeling over him, pounding on his chest and breathing in his mouth as Grace and I stood by helplessly crying in confusion and fear.

Returning to the clearing now was both sad and a little eerie. I felt like I was seeing a movie, like I wasn't living my life but watching it play out on a screen.

"I'll be back," I said, and walked away before Mom could ask me what was wrong.

I passed through the maple trees and carried on a little farther along the creek. The flow of the water gurgled and hissed. A bird called high and shrill. "I miss you, Dad," I said to the forest.

"*Darius*," the wind said as it blew through the maples and ripped a clutch of bright red leaves off their branches.

I jumped in alarm. I'd been much jumpier lately than I'd ever been before—a natural by-product of nearly being murdered by an evil ghost—and the wind had sounded so close to a human voice that I didn't give myself too hard a time for letting it get under my skin. But when I turned I saw it was my mom approaching from behind.

"Sorry if I startled you," she said.

"It's okay. Where's Grace?"

She hooked a thumb over her shoulder, back

toward the clearing. "I asked her to wait while I came and checked on you. You okay?"

"Yeah, I'm fine." And as tough as returning to the clearing was, I meant it—I was fine. "I think Dad would like that we're hiking again." I slipped my backpack off my shoulders and pulled out one of the things I'd brought—a pair of Dad's old hiking gloves. "Do you think...?" I started, then cleared my throat and asked again. "Do you think he'd mind if I wore these?"

Mom smiled and wiped away a tear that had sprung suddenly from her eye. She shook her head. "No. I don't think he'd mind that at all."

I slipped the gloves on then closed my eyes tight. They were a little big for me, but not much.

I sighed and opened my eyes. "Let's go back to Grace."

The wind picked up again. The air felt different somehow, sort of like an electrical charge was flowing beneath the surface of the forest. It was odd.

Mom frowned. Whatever it was, she'd picked up on it, too.

My breath caught in my throat and I had to remind myself to breathe. What had gotten into me? We hurried back to the clearing. Grace was standing on the rock. Her back was to us and she didn't seem to notice that we'd returned. She held something in her hands.

"What do you have there, Grace?" I asked.

She turned suddenly and I saw that she was crying.

And then I saw what she held. "Oh, no," I whispered.

"Grace," Mom said. "You brought your father's urn?"

She nodded and looked at her shoes, embarrassed. "I wanted Dad to be back here, back in this place he loved so much." She sounded a little guilty, a little ashamed and fully resigned to facing the inevitable trouble coming her way. She put the lid back on Dad's urn and gripped the jar as tightly as if it were a life preserver and she was drowning.

"That wasn't your decision to make, Grace," Mom said.

Grace began to cry again, sucking in great gasps of breath between sobs. She hurried to Mom, gave her the urn, and allowed herself to be wrapped up in Mom's arms.

"I'm sorry, I'm sorry, I'm sorry," she said between breaths, her face buried in Mom's stomach. "I just wanted to do something nice for Dad."

Mom shushed her gently and said, "It's all right. There's no need to get so upset. Everything will be fine." She kissed the top of Grace's head then looked around. "I think it's time to go."

Mom handed my sister a tissue, and Grace blew her nose loudly as they left the clearing.

I hung back for a moment, alone. I had to. I had to know for certain, one way or the other. I looked at the rock where Dad had died. Then I noticed for the first time that there was a black shadow, almost like a hole, in front of the maple trees on the far side of the clearing. It was only there for a blink of an eye and then it disappeared, as if a seam between two dimensions had been sewn shut with an invisible thread.

I felt a little queasy, but the feeling soon passed. Had Grace spread some of Dad's ashes and opened a portal? If so, it must have been just a small amount, and the portal had been sealed before anything had escaped the Netherrealm. Maybe everything would be okay. We were lucky.

The forest suddenly grew very quiet. No wind, no water, no animals.

A shiver racked my body, and I hugged my arms around my chest. My teeth chattered, and I exhaled loudly, shocked at the sudden temperature change. My breath clouded the air in front of my face.

Across the clearing, lifeless eyes appeared to leer out at me from among the trees. I blinked, and they were gone. I rubbed my face and peered a little closer; there was definitely nothing there.

It had been my imagination. It must have been. The air warmed slightly and my breath no longer formed misty clouds. The forest seemed to wake up from a short but deep slumber. The wind rustled through the trees, the water gurgled along the stream and birds chirped to one another. "Hey, Mom! Grace!" I shouted. "Wait for me!"

I left the clearing without any further delay, resisting the powerful urge to steal one last glance back over my shoulder.

© Colleen Morris

Joel A. Sutherland is the author of *Be a Writing Superstar*, numerous volumes of the Haunted Canada series (which received the Silver Birch Award and the Hackmatack Award), *Summer's End* (finalist for the Red Maple Award), and *Frozen Blood*, a horror novel that was nominated for the Bram Stoker Award. His short fiction has appeared in many anthologies and magazines, including *Blood Lite II & III* and *Cemetery Dance* magazine, alongside the likes of Stephen

King and Neil Gaiman. He has been a juror for the John Spray Mystery Award and the Monica Hughes Award for Science Fiction and Fantasy.

He is a children's and youth services librarian and appeared as "The Barbarian Librarian" on the Canadian edition of the hit television show *Wipeout*, making it all the way to the third round and proving that librarians can be just as tough and wild as anyone else.

Joel lives with his family in southeastern Ontario, where he is always on the lookout for ghosts.

Read all the books in the Haunted series!

HAUNTED

The
**Nightmare
Next Door**

Joel A. Sutherland

HAUNTED

**Field of
Screams**

Joel A. Sutherland

HAUNTED

**Ghosts
Never Die**

Joel A. Sutherland

HAUNTED

**Night of the
Living Dolls**

Joel A. Sutherland